# LITTLE JAKE'S

## COWDOG

By Gerald (Jake) Conkin

Buckaroo Jake Productions

This book is dedicated
to the memory of our twin sons:
KEVIN LAINE and KORY MARK.
Had they been given the privilege of a full life,
they would have made 'tophands'.

Canadian Cataloguing in Publication Data

Conkin, Jake, 1938-
    Little Jake's Cowdog


ISBN 0-9684444-0-7

    I. Title
PS8555.O5363L57 1999      jC813'.54      C98-911087-7
PZ7.C76Li 1999


Published by:
Buckaroo Jake Productions
S2, C1, RR1
Slocan Park, B.C.
V0G 2E0
Phone: (250) 226-7694
email: buckaroojake@hotmail.com

Typesetting and layout by Laser Graphix
476 Baker Street, Nelson, B.C.  V1L 4H8
ramsays@netidea.com

Printed in Canada by:
Webcom Limited

## ACKNOWLEDGEMENTS:

I'd like to thank Terry Milliken, Tom Dynneson (Rock Creek), Stan Jacobs and the other buckaroos who always made me welcome at the Douglas Lake Cattle Company cowcamps. It is from those experiences that LITTLE JAKE'S COWDOG evolved. Riding with these 'tophands' gave me the special opportunity of experiencing my passion for 'cowboy history'.

A very special thanks to my wife, Carol for spending countless hours, editing and 'keeping me on the trail'.

I chose Ben Crane to do the artwork for this special book. His passion for the buckaroo experience and cowboy culture was needed to add authenticity.

A special hand to Sam and Joan for taking time to 'cold read' and pick the 'stones' out of the pasture.

And a touch of my hat brim to the rest of my family for 'supporting my dreams' as I keep riding the 'buckaroo trail'.

VISIT www.buckaroojake.com FOR MORE BOOKS AND FUN WITH BUCKAROO JAKE

# Double C Ranch
## LAYOUT & MAP

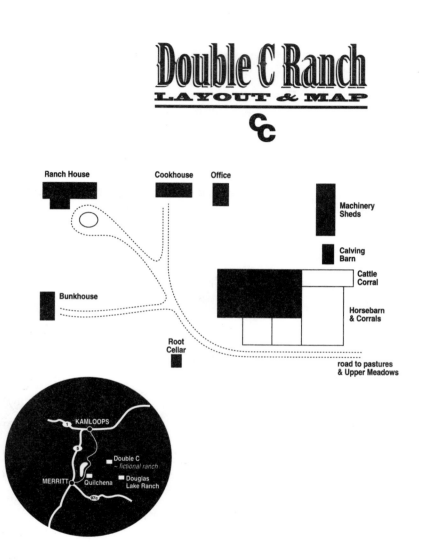

Ranch House

Cookhouse

Office

Machinery Sheds

Calving Barn

Cattle Corral

Bunkhouse

Horsebarn & Corrals

Root Cellar

road to pastures & Upper Meadows

KAMLOOPS

Double C
~ fictional ranch

MERRITT

Quilchena

Douglas Lake Ranch

# ·⋆˙Chapter 1˙⋆·

Little Jake sat on the stairs of the Double C Ranch cookhouse watching a robin and swallow fight over a birdhouse. It was the one that Grandpa and he had built and nailed to the porch. If Grandpa had been there, they would have shared a chuckle over those crazy birds.

Life had sure changed since Grandpa died and he and his mom had come to live on the Ranch.

The early spring sun had just cleared the horizon and its warmth was making his eyelids droop. A cool breeze wafted through - sending a shiver up his back. His eyes opened just in time to keep him from falling off his perch. Grabbing the porch railing, he looked sheepishly over his shoulder, hoping no one had seen him begin his nose dive.

Now wide awake, he found himself staring at a wad of fresh chicken manure in a dustbowl at the bottom of the stairs. He shuddered to think what might have happened if he'd fallen into the smelly mess. "Sheesh, that sun is sure making me drowsy. I'd better smarten up!"

If he'd missed the chicken turds, he would have landed on top of One-Eye, who was curled up twitching and dreaming of chasing gophers.

One-Eye was the oldest cowdog on the Ranch. When he was young, he worked and gathered cattle with the cowboss, Rock Creek. One-Eye didn't go out on the range anymore because his hearing and sight had become impaired.

Rock Creek had retired One-Eye – worried that his loyal working companion would get stomped on by a maverick steer or charged by a tempermental bull. He now used the much younger cowdog, McDuff, who had been Grandpa's cowdog.

These days, One-Eye and Little Jake spent alot of time together. They had become the very best of pals.

Stumbling down the stairs, Little Jake reached out and patted One-Eye on the head.

"You know what, good buddy, I don't want to hurt your feelings, but I need a young pup! You know, one to call my own and train all by myself. You understand, don't you, One-Eye? I really want to....to be a buckaroo, just like Gramps!"

One-Eye gazed up at him and wagged his tail as if to tell Little Jake that he understood and wasn't offended.

# ⋆⋆⋆Chapter 2⋆⋆⋆

He so often thought about all the useful things he'd learned from his Grandpa, even though it was over a year since his passing. Putting his arm around One-Eye, he remembered a conversation they had while on a trip to Merritt - the nearest town.

"Son, you realize, training a cowdog takes time and a lot of patience. You'll have to start your pup on a herd of ducks. Now I say herd instead of flock because we work with herds on a ranch," chuckled Grandpa.

"Fun–ny, Gramps! But why ducks?" asked Little Jake.

"Well, son, a pup is still 'green'. His muscles and bones aren't fully developed so he ain't too agile just yet. He has to practice gatherin' critters that aren't going to get him into a wreck and hurt him. Once he understands the signals and grows bigger, you'll be able to put him on a flock of sheep - oops, I mean a herd of sheep," winked Grandpa.

"Signals? Oh, you mean the whistles and voice commands the buckaroos use. Right?"

"That's right! I'm sure you've heard Rock Creek call out, "That'll do! He wants his cowdog to quit working a cow or the herd and to come back to him. A workin' cowdog has an inbred instinct that makes him want to herd all the time. You know those darn dogs would herd twenty-four hours a day if'n you'd let 'um."

"Wouldn't all that running around wear the dog out, Gramps?"

"Yup, it shure can, son. That's why it's so important to train them right. One of the most important commands that a dog will learn is, "That'll do!"

"Okay, Gramps, I think I understand what you're sayin'."

"That's good, son. Those three words save a lot of dog energy. It's the cowboy's way of sayin', "heel". We like our dogs to walk along at the back of our cowpony until he's needed. Pretty amazing how powerful two words kin be, eh?" he continued.

He also remembered asking his Grandpa if there were other signals he'd have to know when he got his very own cowdog.

"Oh, yes! Of course. Over and above the signals, you'll have to remember to be consistent. Otherwise you'll confuse your pup. A young pup has to hear the exact same words over and over if he's to become a good cowdog.

Now, 'Go-by' orders the dog to circle around the herd in a clockwise direction and 'Away to me' says to circle the herd in a counterclockwise direction. I'll also need to teach you how to use one of those whistles. The whistle is especially important when you lose sight of your dog or he's a distance away from you."

"Gosh!" chuckled Grandpa. "I remember when McDuff was a pup and he tackled some ducks. He tripped over his big paws and tumbled 'bum over tea kettle' into the whole quacking herd! They scattered in a hundred different directions. Poor McDuff, he looked so embarrassed!"

"I sure wish I'd been there to see that!" Little Jake laughed.

"Gramps, what happens after the pup learns to herd the ducks?"

"Sheep, son, sheep. Next come the sheep. After all the Border Collie is the original sheep herder, you know. Once he gets good with sheep, you'll put him on cows. These hounds are worth their weight in gold when it comes to scarin' cows out of the brush. They save a lot of bunged-up buckaroo knees. Let me tell ya! Next to your cowpony, a cowdog will become your most prized possession."

Someday this conversation would help Little Jake train his own cowdogs.

# ⁺₊⁺Chapter 3⁺₊⁺

One-Eye licked Little Jake's freckled hand, bringing him back to the present. He whimpered, wanting Little Jake to pet him. "You know what, One-Eye, you're the best! I do wish you were younger though. Maybe someday I'll be lucky and get a pup just like you. Maybe even from the Waldron Ranch - where you came from. Now wouldn't that be something?"

Rock Creek had told Little Jake about finding One-Eye at the Waldron Ranch in the foothill country of Alberta. It was there that Jack, the manager, raised champion Border Collies.

When Rock Creek visited the Waldron, late one fall, One-Eye was just a little bundle of white and black fuzzy hair. He caught his eye immediately. The pup's colour was different because he had a black patch covering one of his eyes. From a distance, he looked like he only had one eye - the one with the white patch. Without hesitation, Rock Creek decided he should be named, One-Eye!

At eight weeks, he was already herding his brothers and sisters into a corner of their bedding pen. Rock Creek knew right then that he had picked a champ.

"He's the pick of the litter," said Jack. "He's gonna cost you a pair of your fancy chinks*, Rock Creek."

"You drive a hard bargain, Jack! But there's jest no way I'm leavin' here without that pup! I've gotta have'm. He's gonna be the best durn stock dog that's ever chased a cow; let me tell ya!" exclaimed Rock Creek.

One-Eye had lived up to Rock Creek's expectations. He took the place of two hired hands when it came to working in the brush and trees. The only wages he expected were a bowl of crunchy dogfood and anything he could mooch from the cookhouse. It became a ritual for anyone coming out of the cookhouse, to toss a leftover tidbit at One-Eye. If he hadn't worked as hard as he had, he'd have been the fattest dog in the Nicola Valley.

Little Jake really wanted to have a champion cowdog like One-Eye.

The slam of the cookhouse door startled him. It was his mom. She stopped and looked down at him wondering why he seemed so glum. "Why the long face, son?"

"Mom, I really, really need a cowdog! I just have to have one!" he cried.

She seemed puzzled, "Well, you do have One-Eye."

"But, Mom! One-Eye, is not really my dog! We're pals, but he's retired now and Rock Creek doesn't want him to work anymore. We have a lot of fun together but he's not my cowdog, Mom!" Little Jake tried to explain, giving One-Eye a squeeze to make sure he still felt loved.

"Jake, (only Mom ever called him, "Jake") I'm sorry, but I've already told you that I'm too busy trying to keep this ranch 'out of the red'. I don't have time to put up with a new pup right now," she finished, walking down the stairs.

"But, Mom, I'm going to be ten........!" Little Jake's words trailed off as she departed for the ranch office.

"No arguments, Jake! That's my final word!" Was what Little Jake heard as the ranch office door closed behind her.

His head hung between his knees, Little Jake grumbled, "Gee whiz, Mom! Ever since you and Dad divorced and we moved to the Ranch, you're always too busy to listen! I wish Dad was here! He'd understand."

It was times like these, Little Jake missed Dad, who lived in Vancouver.

Little Jake often puzzled over the reason why his mom and dad no longer lived together. He guessed what caused the divorce was that their lives were so different.

His dad was a city person, born and raised in West Vancouver. He had a Masters Degree in Computer Sciences and spent most of his time 'clacking away' on a computer for a software company.

A chuckle escaped Little Jake as he remembered when he was a little tyke, his dad would become so involved with his computer, he'd often forget to put him to bed. And when Mom got home from night classes, Dad always got a scolding!

Little Jake's mom, on the other hand, was born and raised on the Double C Ranch. It was located in the Nicola Valley of south-central British Columbia - the home of some of the largest cattle ranches in Canada.

The Double C had been in the family for three generations. It was one of the larger spreads in the Nicola Valley, running about five thousand head of Hereford-mixed cattle.

Grandpa Jake also raised Registered Quarter Horses and had about fifty head on the Ranch at any one time.

Like most ranch owners, he had been an environmentalist and treated both his land and the government land he leased, with great respect. After all, his livelihood depended on it!

Little Jake recalled a special ceremony everyone from the Ranch attended in Merritt, just before Grandpa died. It was there that he received an environmental award - a bronze plaque in honour of his stewardship of the land. Little Jake had glowed with pride when Grandpa accepted the Award.

Mom was carrying on Grandpa's tradition; the love and care of the land.

The ranch was left to Mom in Grandpa's will. She had a very strong attachment to the Double C and knew it would be a great place for Little Jake to grow up.

Dad, however, insisted he was going to remain in Vancouver. He tried every conceivable way to convince Mom to sell the ranch. Little Jake shuddered, recalling the bitter arguments between them. Finally they agreed that it was best to lead separate lives.

The divorce was very upsetting to Little Jake. However it helped that both parents told him they loved him and that they would all remain friends.

Although he missed Dad and the city, he had Mom, his cowpony, Kasey, One-Eye and Old Smelly.

The goosedown comforter on his bed had been christened 'Old Smelly' by Mom. He giggled about why. Whenever he ate beans, it seemed he could fart forever. It was one of those times when Mom walked in and Old Smelly was loaded!

As she tucked him in, a horrible smell escaped, causing her to gasp and rush out of the bedroom. Pinching her nose, she craned her head around the bedroom door and scolded Little Jake. "You rascal, you're worse than those ill-mannered buckaroos! You'd better make sure you put Old Smelly out on the porch to air," she had said, closing the bedroom door tightly. 🏇

# ⋆⋆⋆Chapter 4⋆⋆⋆

While Grandpa was still alive, Little Jake had always looked forward to visiting the Ranch. Grandpa was one of the best cowhands in the Valley and young Jake wanted to be just like him.

During his visits, Grandpa would take him everywhere he went. Sometimes it was on his dilapidated pickup and other times it would be on horseback. Little Jake learned many things about being a cowboy from his Grandpa. When he was with him, he was a 'buckaroo in training'!

He especially liked to go into Merritt with Grandpa. As they travelled into town, Grandpa would tell him about the history of the Nicola Valley and point out historic landmarks along the way.

Whenever they drove out onto the Douglas Lake Road, Little Jake always asked about an old sod-roofed cabin built by one of the first ranchers in the Nicola Valley - way back in the 1800's. "You know, Gramps, I still can't figure out how it is that a roof made out of dirt with grass growing out of it, doesn't leak." he would say.

"You're goin' to wear me out trying to explain it, you young buck!" Grandpa, always replied, as he playfully punched him on the shoulder.

Trundling along Douglas Lake Road, they often saw wildlife. Occasionally, even bears lumbered along the grassy slopes near the highway. One time, they were surprised when a fat, glossy-coated brown bear raced along the fence line in the same direction they were going.

Grandpa decided to clock the bear's speed on his speedometer. "Gee Willikers, son, he's doin' close to fifty kilometers per hour! That hairy rascal could outrace a good cowpony. Hee! Hee!" Grandpa had laughed, as he gunned the engine and passed the panting bear!

Little Jake had turned to look out the back window. "Gramps, he went through the fence. He's crossed the road and crashed into the buckbrush along the Nicola River, boy that was cool!"

Little Jake always looked for the log church belonging to the Upper Nicola Indian Band. Once he'd spotted the church's spire, he knew they were near the main highway. The church was nestled at the end of Douglas Lake Road framed by glistening Nicola Lake. It wouldn't be long before they whizzed by the historic Quilchena Hotel and General Store - one of Little Jake's favourite stopping places.

In Merritt, the first stop was Andy's Saddleshop. Whenever Andy heard Grandpa's pickup rattle into the parking lot, he'd start pouring two cups of very strong cowboy coffee. Anticipating another long chin wag with Old Jake, Andy prepared his usual sarcastic greeting. After that was over, they'd settle into talking about leather, saddles and arguing about who in the Valley had the best cowpony.

While they visited, Little Jake got a chance to look at all the great buckaroo gear in the shop. He drooled over a pair of red and black hightop boots, hoping nobody would buy them until his feet grew into them.

He also admired a Stetson hanging high up on the wall. Andy's cashier, Wendy, would say, "Hey, wanna try on that silverbelly agin', Little Jake?"

It was fun looking into the mirror and seeing that great looking Stetson covering his blond curls, which he insisted should be cut very short. He wiggled his up-turned, freckled nose and grinned into the mirror.

Mom always teased him about his nose, but he was

proud of his nose, which he had inherited from his beloved Grandpa!

After leaving the Saddle Shop, they crossed the small bridge over the Nicola River and headed down Voght Street to the Coldwater Hotel - a heritage landmark in Merritt. It was a grand building with ornate wooden porches and a copper-domed tower which could be seen for miles around. This was a favourite stop for buckaroos on their occasional trip to town.

Like most buckaroos, Grandpa enjoyed a beer. He liked to sneak into the hotel for a 'quick one'. As he left the pickup, Grandpa would hold his finger up to his lips to swear Little Jake to secrecy. He would return with a mischevious grin and lift the very same finger to remind Little Jake of their secret.

On the way home, they would finally reach the legendary Quilchena Hotel. Grandpa would gear down as they bounced over the potholes in the parking lot.

"Well, son, I see those old long-winded, stove-up* buckaroos, Charlie, Joe, and Pete are here. You'd think they had nothin' better to do than hang around drinkin' coffee and fillin' their bellies," he would say, shaking his head.

He always knew which of his cronies were at the Hotel by their beat-up pickups. "The one with the gumbo* paint job is Pete's. If they were givin' out prizes for the ugliest pickup in the Valley, he'd win for shure. Yep, he would!" he would chortle.

"I kin bet they'll be gettin' to repeatin' those same old stories agin', too. And then they'll go to tellin' how smart and good lookin' they are!" he always complained. "I just don't know why I keep stoppin' here!" Grandpa would go on.

Little Jake would chuckle knowing that Grandpa really loved trying to outdo his buddies with his own special brand of tall tales. And Grandpa was also one of the worst for repeating stories. He always gave as good as he got!

Instead of heading for the dining room, Little Jake would sneak into the Saloon and search for the bullets embedded in the bar.

Imagining an actual gunfight, he would become one of the gunslingers. Just as he'd be about to pull the trigger on his six-gun, Grandpa's gravelly voice would interrupt his day dream. "Hey there, Pistol Pete, you'd better get in here and put in your order."

After his usual delicious burger and fries, Little Jake felt plumb full, but he always left room for dessert. This was never ordered at the Hotel because they went over to the General Store and Post Office for a large double-dip ice cream cone.

Robin, the store manager, enjoyed chatting with Little Jake and made sure he got an extra dollop of his favourite - double chocolate chip. Carrying an armload of mail as they left, Little Jake would struggle to keep the big dollop of ice cream from hitting the dirt.

Once in the pickup, Grandpa muttered as he struggled with his seatbelt. "Click! Click!" And then the engine roared. They soon rattled out onto the pavement towards home.

A short distance past Quilchena, Grandpa would crank the steering wheel hard to the right onto a very dusty, gravel washboard. This way home took them past Dry Farm cowcamp and Minnie Lake. The truck would fish-tail and rattle up the hill onto the rangeland plateau as Grandpa changed gears and sped up.

"That's sure hard on these old kidneys," Grandpa would groan, twisting and turning in his seat, trying to get comfortable. To keep his mind off his aches and pains, he'd begin to reminisce about the 'good ol' days'. Grandpa loved to talk about the time he was a young buckaroo on the 'big outfits' - one of the biggest being the Douglas Lake Cattle Company.

"I was only sixteen when I left home and hired on. I was pretty big for my age so I told the manager I was eighteen. Yep! I was the youngest buck on that outfit," he always began, looking over to see his grandson's reaction.

Little Jake then questioned Grandpa about his 'fib', but all Grandpa said was, "Well, son, it was only a little 'fib'...and now that I've gotten older, I don't 'fib' anymore!" Then he'd look out of the corner of his eye, to see if Little Jake actually believed him. "Well, maybe just an occasional tall tale, son. You know, just when I'm around those word-stretchin' old galoots!"

Little Jake had heard Grandpa's stories so often that he would mouth the words right along with him. "Did you say somethin', son?" Grandpa always asked; noticing Little Jake's lips moving.

"Nope! Not really, Gramps," fibbed Little Jake, playing Grandpa's game and trying to keep a straight face.

Once when they had been bumping along past Dry Farm cowcamp, Grandpa swerved suddenly and headed for the 'toolies'*. "Sheesh, Gramps!" hollered Little Jake, bouncing into him - his hat landing on the pickup floor. "That one beer you had at the Coldwater Hotel is sure making you do strange things!"

As soon as he said it, Little Jake realized he'd made a mistake. Grandpa was struggling with the steering wheel wrenching the wheel hard to get the pickup back out of the loose gravel. Dirt was rooster-tailing off the back wheels and a cloud of dust settled over them. With the truck back on the road, Grandpa gave Little Jake a stern look. Little Jake knew what it was for.

"Sorry, Gramps. I was just trying to be funny," he apologized.

"Now doncha' go to preachin' at your Grandpa like your Grandma used to, you hear!" said Grandpa, reaching out and giving Little Jake a playful cuff on the ear. "Apology accepted! Now if'n you weren't so busy mouthin' off and had looked out your side mirror, you'd have seen why I headed for the toolies!"

Glancing at the side mirror, Little Jake spotted a coyote disappearing into a grove of aspens, near the edge of the road. "Now there's a cowdog for yuh, son," laughed Grandpa. He'd make a good 'un," he teased.

"Oh, sure, Gramps!" mumbled Little Jake, not appreciating Grandpa fooling with him. 🐎

# ⋆⁺⋆Chapter 5⋆⁺⋆

Every day he'd spent at the Ranch had been a new learning experience for Little Jake. He helped fix fences, shoe horses, doctor cattle. And although it was a yucky job, in the springtime, Little Jake even helped deliver calves.

The early spring of the year that Grandpa had passed away, Little Jake learned how to use a calf-puller.

He and Mom had been at the ranch one weekend when Grandpa woke him up around midnight. "Get up, son! Here's your chance to learn a very important buckaroo skill!"

Rubbing the sleep out of his eyes, his shirt-tails still hanging out of his Levis, Little Jake stumbled into the calving shed. Grandpa was holding a lethal-looking contraption made of metal bars and chains. A heifer was having trouble delivering her first calf. Little Jake swallowed hard and stepped in behind Grandpa, not wanting to get too close. "Is this going to be very messy, Gramps," he asked, quite concerned.

"Alright, son, hold onto this lever while I get the chains untangled. When I tell you to work that lever, get on it real fast, you hear?" ordered Grandpa, as he prepared to help the heifer.

"Yes, Gramps." sputtered Little Jake, grasping the lever tightly with both hands. He turned his head away, hoping he wouldn't have to look. He held his breath as long as he could to keep out the stench. "Yuckers!" he blurted, hoping Grandpa didn't hear.

"Here it comes, son. Work that lever some more."

"Great! Son! That's great! You did that like a tophand. You just helped save a life," complimented Grandpa.

Little Jake had delivered his first calf. This made him feel grown-up and important. And a big step closer to being a bonafide buckaroo!

He felt his stomach churn as he watched Grandpa pull the membrane and mucus from the calf's mouth and nostrils. Within moments the newborn twitched, snorted and tried to get up on his spindly, wobbly legs. Weaving back and forth, like a drunken sailor, he fell down again and again. Grandpa and Little Jake chuckled at the clownish antics of the baby bull.

Little Jake hoped he was finished and was thinking about his cosy bed. Just as he stepped out of the calving shed, he was stopped by Grandpa calling. "Hey, are you still there?"

"What now?" wondered Little Jake. Covering a big yawn with his hand, he turned reluctantly and shuffled back into the shed. "Over here, son. Rock Creek says we've got a 'Caesarean' on our hands."

"But, that's a job for a vet, isn't it, Gramps? I'm no vet," Little Jake said, hoping to be 'let off the hook' so he could get back to bed.

"Oh, I realize that, son, but we might need you to give us a hand. So 'stick around', willya," replied Grandpa.

Rock Creek had walked in with a small metal case. As he opened it, Little Jake saw tools that looked like they belonged to a doctor. "You may not be a vet, but if you want to be a buckaroo one day, you'll have to do this too," he explained, as he got a scalpel ready. "Come over here, young fellah." Warily, Little Jake inched toward Rock Creek.

"You see, this calf is much too big to come out the normal way, so we've got to cut the belly of the mother cow to get that calf out," said Grandpa.

As much as Little Jake didn't want to look, his curiosity took over and he looked as Rock Creek began to cut. "Gross me out!" he muttered, as his tummy did cartwheels once again. He ran out the door and 'dropped his cookies'. Hanging onto the handle of the shed door, he heaved and shook, for what seemed like forever.

Little Jake felt something on his shoulder. It was Rock Creek's hand. Crouching down, Rock Creek looked up at him and smirked. He didn't say anything but continued to wipe his mucky hands with a rag. The sight of the blood and the smell of the rag caused a final gut-wrenching dry heave to come out of Little Jake. He was feeling so miserable! All he wanted was to be left alone.

"Well, young fellah," cackled Rock Creek. "I see youse don't take too kindly to the most exciting part of bein' a buckaroo. Hee! Hee!" he cackled again and strolled back to help Grandpa suture the belly of the mother cow.

Green and holding onto his tummy, Little Jake, took a deep breath and sidled back into the shed. "I guess I'd better prove to Gramps and Rock Creek that I can watch the rest of this. Leaving now wouldn't be the 'buckaroo way'. Rock Creek would never let me live it down," he thought, as he wandered back in.

# ✦Chapter 6✦

Little Jake and Mom had always spent their summers at the Ranch. There was a particular day about a year ago that he'll never forget. Grandpa had been up early as usual. He had a doctor's appointment in Merritt that day. But before he left for Merritt, he insisted he had to check on a bull he had doctored for foot rot a few days before.

Hearing Grandpa calling McDuff, woke Little Jake. He thought about getting up and riding out with him, but his eyes just wouldn't stay open. One eyelid lifted just enough to see that daybreak had arrived.

The goosedown comforter felt especially cozy that morning. Rolling over, he pulled Old Smelly over the top of his head. He wiggled and kicked to rebuild his nest. Ducking under the covers, he blew a fart and giggled to himself!

Now that Grandpa had found McDuff, he grabbed a rope from the back of his pickup and walked into the horse corral.

"Doolie! Doolie!" he called. "Over here, old timer." Doolie answered with a nicker. He was so well trained that whenever Grandpa held up an open loop, the old cowpony walked over and stuck his head into it. This was one of the ways Grandpa bragged about how well-trained his cowpony was - especially whenever a buckaroo was nearby!

As Grandpa brushed Doolie, McDuff sat on his haunches and waited patiently - eager to get out on the range. For some strange reason, when Grandpa brushed Doolie, McDuff always sat right next to Doolie's hind leg.

It never failed that Doolie let loose a load of manure and 'in the nick of time', McDuff barely escaped getting dumped on!

Grandpa marvelled at McDuff's ability to sense what was about to happen. "He'll get you yet, McDuff," smirked Grandpa. "If nothing else, you're great for starting off my day with a good laugh."

Lifting his heavy saddle onto Doolie's back, he felt a jab of pain in his chest. "Darn! I guess I'd better get this job done and get into Merritt to see the Doc," he said, leaning against Doolie to catch his breath.

The sun had been up for several hours when Little Jake headed for breakfast. He wished he'd gotten up earlier and gone with Grandpa.

Cramming his mouth full of cereal, he heard something scratching at the screen door. He stopped chewing and listened. Not swallowing, he swung his legs over the bench and turned the doorknob. It was McDuff! "What are you doing here?" blurted Little Jake, spraying McDuff with cereal. "Why, aren't you with Gramps?"

Hearing the word, Gramps, made McDuff whine. He darted off the porch and ran towards the roadway leading to the Upper Meadows. Little Jake turned his eyes toward the horsebarn and didn't see anyone. He was sure Grandpa wouldn't be back so soon. McDuff ran back to Little Jake and whined again. He then ran back past the horse corrals and onto the roadway. "What are you trying to tell me, McDuff? Is something wrong? You're acting very strange," he shouted.

The third time McDuff came back, he stood up on his hind legs and placed his front paws on Little Jake's chest. This time he let out a howl, making Little Jake stagger backwards.

Pushing McDuff off, Little Jake sped towards the

horsebarn. "Gramps! Gramps!" he called. There was no response! McDuff was back up on the roadway - barking loudly. It was as if he was saying, "Please, Little Jake, follow me!"

McDuff was so persistent, Little Jake was now sure that something must have happened to Grandpa. Panic-stricken, he raced back to the ranch office! "Mom, come quick! Something's terribly wrong! McDuff is back without Gramps! A.a.a.a.and he's trying to get me to follow him," he cried.

Turning pale, she fumbled for her jacket and rushed out into the ranch yard.

"Jake, we don't have time to saddle up. Run over to the machine shed and start up the Jeep," she ordered. "I'll get the First Aid Kit."

McDuff sensed that his message had finally been understood and ran to join Little Jake in the Jeep. Tears welled up in Little Jake's eyes. "Please, please, let Gramps be okay! Please, please let Gramps be okay! Why didn't I get up and ride out with him?" he asked himself, regretfully.

He grabbed the steering wheel and yanked himself onto the seat. Forgetting to put his foot on the clutch, he turned the key. The Jeep lurched forward and crashed into a stack of straw bales, sending a flock of old nesting hens squawking. Feathers flew everywhere!

Flailing at the loose straw covering his head, Little Jake picked an old hen off his lap and threw her out. He shook his head and tried to collect himself.

A bale of straw had landed on the hood blocking his vision. McDuff cowered on the Jeep's floorboard. With The Jeep now stalled, he got up, gave himself a shake and leapt into the rear jumpseat. It was obvious he felt a whole lot safer there.

This time, Little Jake remembered to put his foot on the clutch. Jerking his way out of the mess of straw and broken eggs, the Jeep roared out of the shed.

"Are you alright, son?" Mom asked, as she tripped into the driver's seat, forcing Little Jake to scramble to the other side.

"I'm okay, Mom!" he replied , still fishing straw out of his shirt and using it to wipe the mess the hen had left on his jeans. McDuff leaped onto Little Jake's lap, feeling more secure now that Mom was driving. But Little Jake shoved him back into the rear seat. With the sound of grinding gears, roaring engine and squawking chickens, they screeched out of the ranch yard.

Mom drove like a banshee! Little Jake clutched the roll bar so tightly his knuckles turned white, while McDuff bounced around like a rag doll!

They fish-tailed through the meadows searching for a sign of Grandpa. Blasting over the top of a knoll, Little Jake grabbed the rollbar with one hand and the top of the windshield with the other so he could stand up to see better. He spotted Doolie!

Nearby a bull sniffed at something in the bunchgrass. "Did Grandpa get gored by the bull?" His heart did a double flip as he pointed out where she should go.

Blowing the horn to scare the bull away, she brought the Jeep to a grinding halt! Simultaneously, they spotted Grandpa lying face down! At first glance, it looked like he had stopped to lay down for a rest. "Oh, No!" she screamed.

Asking Little Jake to help her roll Grandpa over onto his back, she gently called, "Dad" a number of times.

A shudder passed through Little Jake as he watched his mom put her ear against Grandpa's chest. When she lifted her head, Grandpa's vest was stained with tears.

She couldn't detect a heartbeat!

Quickly, she searched for a pressure point on his wrist—there was no pulse! She lifted Grandpa's chin and opened his mouth. She put the heels of her hands on his chest and made a number of quick compressions, hoping to get the heart to respond. Blowing air into his mouth, nothing happened! Grandpa didn't stir! Little Jake's eyes blurred with tears.

Mom repeated the steps for a long time before she gave up! She looked up at Little Jake and shook her head back and forth. Exhausted, she began to sob uncontrollably!

He reached out and put his arms around her, trying his best to provide comfort! She, in turn, hugged him tightly. They both wept a flood of tears!

A wimpering McDuff snuggled up against Little Jake sensing that something was terribly wrong!

Michelle tried to regain her composure wanting to be strong for Little Jake. She knew how devastated he would be by the death of his best pal, Gramps!✶

# Chapter 7

She placed her hands on Little Jake's slumped shoulders and said, "Jake, I really need you to help me right now. I need you to take the Jeep and go to Paintbrush Meadows and see if you can find Rock Creek? He needs to be here to give us a hand." Little Jake's body felt numb all over and tears kept blurring his vision.

He knew this was something Mom really needed him to do. McDuff and Little Jake lurched and jarred their way through the Upper Meadows scattering gophers and grouse in all directions. This time, nothing slowed the Jeep! Not even rotten deadfalls, rocks nor ditches! They bounced over and through them all.

He found Rock Creek, Pegasus, Forty Mile, and the rest of the crew busy doctoring cows.

Not sure how he'd tell Rock Creek without blubbering out of control, Little Jake braced himself.

Hearing the roaring engine of the Jeep and spotting Little Jake as the driver, Rock Creek sensed something was wrong! He threw the end of his rope to Pegasus and loped toward the bouncing Jeep. Just as he came to a sliding stop, Little Jake scrambled out of the Jeep and flung himself against Rock Creek.

"What is it, little buddy?"

"It's Gramps...Upper Mead...," was all that Little Jake could get out.

"Forty, get on over here!" ordered Rock Creek. "Somethin' bad's happened to the old man! We'll take the Jeep! Let's get a move on!" Rock Creek slid into the driver's seat and Forty jumped in beside him. Lifting McDuff, Little Jake slid onto the jump seat and hung on for dear life. He knew with Rock Creek driving they'd not be wasting any time.

The next couple of days at the Home Ranch were a blur! All that Little Jake remembered were a lot of people coming and going. It was a gloomy time!

Little Jake tried to stay out of everyone's way and did extra chores to help out and keep his mind occupied. He didn't sleep well for many nights! But it helped seeing his dad again. At least now, he had someone to talk to.

He had never been to a funeral before. His Grandma passed away when he was too young to remember. The only way, Little Jake had experienced death before was when a ranch animal died. He was old enough to realize that dying was something that happened to all living things. But, that didn't make it any easier, when someone as special as Gramps was gone!

Grandpa Jake Corbin Sr. was buried on a knoll beside Grandma Effie, overlooking his beloved Double C Ranch.

He still found it difficult to accept his passing. "It's not fair! I really miss you, Gramps! You'll always be my very best pal!"

# ·⋆·Chapter 8·⋆·

Several days after Mom refused to let him have a cow-dog, Little Jake was mucking out the horsebarn and Rock Creek rode by. "Hey young fellah, meet me out back at the horse corrals."

Little Jake was suspicious of Rock Creek's invitation. He knew he had a reputation for being a 'practical joker'! He wondered what Rock Creek had 'up his sleeve' this time. Leaning the manure fork against a stall, he gave his dusty jeans a thwack with his Stetson and ambled over to the horse corrals.

"Hey, guy, over here. Hang in a minute, while I brush down my bronc," said Rock Creek, pleased to see that Little Jake had showed up.

"Shure!" answered Little Jake, still suspicious of Rock Creek's motives.

Rock Creek motioned Little Jake in a little closer and said, "We shure do miss your Grandpa around here, Little Jake. He was one of the best cowboys I ever rode with and the best boss I ever worked fer! I learned a whole bunch from him.....'specially 'bout good horses. He always treated me right and I guess that's why I've stayed on at the Double C till I wore out two saddles! He must've known somethin' was wrong with his ticker, though."

"One day, way back, your Grandpa told me, Rock Creek, if anythin' should ever happen to me, I want you to keep an eye on that young cowpoke of ours. Make sure you keep'em learnin' everythin' about becomin' a 'top-hand'. An' when he's learned all the important stuff, you get him saddled and out with the rest of those buckaroos.

And on occasion, get'm up to the cowcamps and out on the range helpin' wherever he kin."

"Well, the way I figgers it - it's gettin' to be about thet time! How's that sound to yuh?"

"Rea–lly? Does that mean I can—!" squealed Little Jake.

"Yup," interrupted Rock Creek. That's exactly what I mean!"

Little Jake reached out to 'high five' Rock Creek, and spooked his cowpony. "Whoa, there horse! Aincha ever seen a jumpin' bean cowpoke before?" grinned Rock Creek, as he grabbed for the halter shank. When Little Jake hit the barn floor, he was already galloping off toward the ranch office.

"What? Mom's not here! I hope she's in the cook-house," mumbled Little Jake, as he slammed the screen door and sprinted for the cookhouse.

One-Eye, awoke with a start as Little Jake thundered past. Leaping up, he caught him with a big slurpy kiss. "Oh, One-Eye! Yuck! I shure didn't need that," he complained.

He found his mom having coffee and a piece of hot apple pie with Sharon, the ranch cook. The entire cook-house was filled with the delicious aroma of apple pie.

"Guess what, Mom! Rock Creek just told me that I'm ready to ride with the cowboy crew!" Throwing up his arms, he nearly knocked her piece of pie off the table.

Rescuing her pie and setting her fork down, Michelle reached out and gave him a big hug. "Yahoo! buckaroo! "Congratulations!

You were so lucky to have had a Grandpa that gave you so much of his time. My, he'd be proud of you! You know, son, his spirit will always ride with you," she nodded, putting her arms around his shoulders.

Releasing himself from Mom's grasp, Little Jake sashayed back to the horsebarn. He was feeling mighty grown up!

"Well, I'll sell my saddle if'n those eyes of your'n ain't bigger than a boogered* bronc's! What did your mom say?" asked Rock Creek.

Still quivering with excitement, Little Jake's grin stretched from ear to ear. "With some saddle miles on yuh, you're gonna make a darn good hand one day - just like that Grandpa of yourn'," Rock Creek praised, wheeling a manure cart out of the horse barn.

Little Jake's enthusiasm was soon dampened as he remembered, "But, I'll be the only cowhand without a cowdog! I really do need a cowdog!"

# -*·*Chapter 9·*·*

That night, the Big Dipper spilled millions of stars into the dark sky. The light from a full moon poured into Little Jake's bedroom. He crawled under Old Smelly, still worrying about not having a cowdog.

Tossing and turning continuously, he wondered how he could convince his mom. Scrunching his eyelids tight, he turned away from the moonlight that trickled through his window. Sleep just wouldn't come.

A howling coyote added to his restlessness. His eyes were wide open as he rolled onto his back and listened. "He sure sounds close! It sounds like he's near the horse corrals. He's probably trying to get at those old hens."

The howling was beginning to annoy him. He tried to blot out the sound by scrunching Old Smelly over his ears. "Just what I needed, I can't sleep and now a coyote is howling in my ear."

"I may as well get up and see if I can scare that noisy critter away. "What a nuisance!" he babbled on. His eyes blinking, he stumbled out onto the ranch house porch. The moon was so bright that it lit up the whole ranch yard. Leaning against a porch pillar, he yawned and rubbed his eyes as he tried to focus. He spotted movement near the horse barn. He froze!

"Huh, it looks like two coyotes out there." Whatever the two shapes were they were chasing about and running circles around the barn. They also darted in and out of the horse corrals. As he continued to watch, Little Jake was sure one of the shapes was One-Eye!

"Is One-Eye playing with a coyote? Naw! That's not

possible! It sure looks like One-Eye, though. That's him alright! I can just make out the black patch on his right eye," he whispered. "Wait 'til I tell, Mom. I can't believe that One-Eye would actually be playing with a coyote! I know she won't believe me."

Still glued to the spot, Little Jake continued to watch with astonishment! "Boy, are they ever having fun. A dog and a coyote - friends? I wonder how long this has been going on?"

"Maybe that's why One-Eye's been away from the cookhouse so much. He's been sneaking off to play with that coyote. Maybe he was lonely! All the other cowdogs are out at cowcamps or in the bunkhouse. That's it!" he exclaimed.

Crawling back into his bunk, cowdogs and coyotes chased around in his head. He awoke with a start when the ranch alarm clock - the barn rooster screeched his early morning cock-a-doodle-doo! "Yikes! Too bad that coyote didn't get you last night!" Little Jake grumbled.

Giving his head a shake, he tried to erase the weird dream he'd had about a dog and coyote chasing around the barnyard. He remembered getting up to try to scare away the coyote and then discovering the coyote playing with One-Eye.

"Geesh! I just know no one will believe me. "Hmmm! Maybe I should follow One-Eye and see where he goes when he leaves the ranch yard? Actually, now that I think about it, he's seldom around the cookhouse anymore. I wonder if he actually visits the coyote?" The more he thought about it, the more convinced he became! "If I can prove it, everybody will have to believe that it's possible for a dog and a coyote to be friends!"

Flipping out of his bunk, Little Jake got dressed and headed for breakfast. Stepping off the ranchhouse porch, he noticed One-Eye snoozing in his favourite place - the upper step of the cookhouse.

"I'll bet he thinks he's one crafty cowdog."

As Little Jake approached, One-Eye got up, wagged his tail, stretched and then leapt up planting a slurpy kiss on Little Jake. Once again, catching him off guard.

He dragged his raspy tongue right across Little Jake's lips. "Yuck! Fooey! Yuckers," he sputtered, sticking his elbow out to ward off further affections. "Okay, One-Eye! Now lay off, will yuh. All this mushy stuff isn't going to keep me from finding out what you were doing with that coyote last night," he warned. Happy with the attention he was getting, One-Eye wagged his tail furiously, setting off a miniature dust tornado. Then he lay down, put his paws over his ears and proceeded to ignore Little Jake. It was as if he knew he'd been caught and didn't want to hear about it.◠

# ᛫᛭᛫Chapter 10᛫᛭᛫

Little Jake had breakfast in a hurry so he could keep track of One-Eye. He also quickly packed a bag lunch in case he had to follow him into the hills. An apple, some cheese, and a chunk of roast from last night's supper filled a plastic bread bag.

His mind occupied with his secret mission, he bounded out of the cookhouse and tripped over One-Eye. He hurtled down the stairs- flinging his lunchbag into the yard.

Landing face first in a chicken dustbowl, he pushed himself up ever so slowly. He smelled and then spotted fresh chicken manure across the front of his shirt. The stench made his nose curl even more! He tried to hold his breath - but it was no use! "Phew! That's gross!" he bellowed.

Wrestling his shirt off his back, he stood half-naked as he watched One-Eye devour the dumped roast and cheese. "One-Eye, you dumb galoot! You tripped me up on purpose, didn't you?"

Swishing his shirt at One-Eye, he rescued the remains of the roast and an apple. Dust-covered lunchbag in one hand and a smelly shirt in the other, Little Jake shuffled over to the ranchhouse for a clean shirt.

Snapping the final button closed, Little Jake decided his best vantage point for spying on One-Eye, would be the horsebarn hayloft.

Kneeling on the soft, loose hay, he strained to see through a knothole. Little Jake had to squint because the hole was so small. His sleepless night was catching up with him. His eyelids felt heavy. Before he knew it, his body folded into the pile of soft hay and he dozed off.

Milling, squealing horses in the corral below the hayloft, woke him. Realizing that he'd lost track of One-Eye, he jumped up to look through the knothole and banged his head. "Ow! Ow! Ouch!" he moaned, rubbing his forehead with the heel of his hand. Squinting through the knothole, he spotted One-Eye running over the top of a knoll. Within moments, the small black dot disappeared. "I sure lucked out that time! At least now I know what direction he goes in," said Little Jake, satisfied that his effort wasn't totally lost.

Jumping off the third rung of the loft ladder, Little Jake rushed to grab his saddle. Using his other hand to grab a blanket and headstall, he hurried to the horse corrals. He came around the horse barn so quickly, he boogered his cowpony, Kasey.

Her registered name was Beth Tivio but Grandpa had nicknamed her Kasey because she acted so much like a pup he once owned. Two days after she was born, Grandpa came around the corner of the horsebarn and found Beth Tivio crouched down on her long wobbly legs, daring a bunch of hens and a rooster to pass by. Casey, the blue heeler pup, had done the exact same thing. "Since you act so much like that pup, Beth Tivio, I guess I'll just have to call you Kasey for short!" And he did!

Kasey had been enjoying a stand-up nap and hadn't been expecting anyone. "Oops, I should know better," Little Jake reminded himself.

She ran around the corral refusing to let him catch her. He finally had to take his rope off his saddle and flip a hoolihan* to stop her. Even after she was haltered and tied to the snubbing post, she kept swinging her backside

33

away as Little Jake tried to throw the saddle on.

Exasperated, he tied her to a corral railing and forced her against the corral so that she couldn't side-step away. Finally with the saddle on, they headed out to the Upper Meadows - where he'd last seen One-Eye.

Kasey continued to be obstinate. She just wouldn't listen to Little Jake. He was having trouble keeping her from running off with him. Putting her in tight circles to slow her down became annoying and wasted time - they weren't making much headway.

It seemed to take forever to arrive at the top edge of the Upper Meadows. He slipped out of the saddle and glanced around for a sign of One-Eye. Nothing! Absolutely, nothing! He was nowhere to be seen! "Now where could that darn dog be?" he said in bewilderment, clutching his Stetson in one hand and scratching his head with the other.

Leaving Kasey tied to an aspen sapling, he decided to look around the outer fringes of the Upper Meadows.

An old Bull Pine snag lay across the top of a hill, to his left. The tree was enormous in size and had fallen over from old age. A big hole had been left where the roots had pulled out.

"Gee, that looks like a great spot for a badger - or, hey, maybe a coyote den. It could even be the home of One-Eye's fuzzy-tailed friend," guessed Little Jake.

He took halting steps towards the snag for a closer look. "If it's a badger hole - that could mean trouble! I remember seeing a cowdog ripped up by one. Their claws are something else." He trembled, imagining being attacked by one. "Those critters don't back away from anything."

A high-pitched screech startled Little Jake, diverting his attention upward. His eyes were drawn to the beauty of a large bird floating effortlessly in the bright blue sky. It was a large hawk. The bird was probably searching for its dinner - perhaps a careless gopher.

Little Jake wondered if the hawk had a nest in the large Cottonwood trees near Billy Miner Lake, about a mile from where he stood. "Maybe, when I'm not busy with my secret mission, Kasey and I will ride over there."

Staring up into the sky was making him dizzy. As he brought his head down, his eyes landed on the large Bull Pine snag. Deciding he should make himself less conspicuous, he got down on his knees and inched his way towards the snag. As he got nearer, his adrenalin really started pumping! His hands felt clammy and sweat beaded under his hatband. "I wonder what lives down in that hole? What if it attacks me?" he shuddered, 'his imagination working overtime'.

"Gramps told me, "If a wild critter ever bites you - you could get rabies." Panicked, Little Jake pushed away from the snag. He seriously contemplated making a dash for Kasey.

"I guess I should forget about this whole stupid idea! But that wouldn't be 'the buckaroo way' - now would it? Buckaroos finish what they start- don't they Gramps?" he whispered, half-expecting to receive an answer. He rested for a moment, built up his courage and re-thought his plan of action.

He soon decided he needed protection. Searching the ground around him, he found a thick pine branch. With it tightly grasped in his fist, he felt more secure. Standing up, he reversed his direction back towards the snag.

He held the branch in front of him as he approached. In close, he noticed what looked like dog tracks in the fine dust at the base of the snag. He searched for long claw prints - the sign of a badger. There weren't any. "Thank

Goodness! That means it isn't a badger's hole!" he sighed in relief.

Leaning over, still tense and on guard, he examined the tracks more closely. He noticed that they were of two different sizes. "Hmmm, they sure look like dog tracks but there is a difference. That one set of tracks could be One-Eye's and maybe the other set belongs to a coyote. I'll bet my saddle that my hunch is right," he thought, pleased with his detective work.

"Yep! This could be a coyote den, alright. But, that's as close as I get until I know for sure! Maybe what I'd better do is go get what's left of that roast. I'll break it into pieces and drop it around those tracks and then I'll hide and see what happens."

Scattering the few pieces of roast, Little Jake backed away from the the mound, keeping his eyes on the bait. Crouched down in the bunchgrass, he took off his Stetson and peeked through the stems of grass. He waited and waited! If an animal was nearby, it showed no interest in the bait.

Little Jake's elbows were getting sore and he had a crick in his neck. He was torn between watching and needing to check on Kasey. She had been tied up for a long time. He knew that when she became bored, she dug holes with her front hoof. "I wonder if she's dug a hole to China yet?" he joked.

The day had gotten warm and the air was very still. The flies had become unbearable! They were getting into Little Jake's ears, eyes and even up his nose. There were little black flies, horseflies and deer flies buzzing around his head. He flailed and slapped, hoping they would leave him alone. "Darn, you pesky bugs!" he complained. He knew the flies would be chewing on Kasey too!

He convinced himself to stay for a few more minutes.

Nothing moved except the flies. Suddenly his attention was diverted upward - a familiar shrieking sound pierced the silence and made him flip over and gaze up into the sky. "So there are two of you! A Mr. and Mrs. Hawk! That means you must be nesting in those cottonwoods near Billy Miner Lake. I'm gonna have to get over there and check it out," he concluded.

He found it fascinating to watch the hawks do graceful, swooping spirals in the warm air currents. "Sure wish I could float around like that! That way I would always know where One-Eye was!"

"Well, so much for that. I guess I'd better be going! Nothing seems to be happening out here, anyway." Turning to leave, Little Jake took a final glance at where he'd left the bait.

"Oh, no! Just my luck!" he exclaimed. "There's a crow! That ugly beady-eyed bird is after the meat. That'll wreck my whole plan! Shoo! You pest! Shoo!" he shouted, waving his Stetson.

Suddenly, one of the hawks dropped out of the sky. It was low enough for Little Jake to see its shimmering feathers. Just as he cupped his fingers around his eyes for a better look, the hawk let out a piercing screech and dove.

"Oh, no! Now it's going to snatch the meat! He's going to steal it! Little Jake covered his eyes and stood mesmerized! A blood-curdling screech caused him to peek through his fingers! "Jeepers! He's got the crow!" With a diving swoop, the hawk flew off with the crow tightly clutched in its talons - black feathers scattering everywhere.

"Aw, right, Mr.Hawk! Way to go! That pesky crow won't steal my bait again! Thanks, Mr. Hawk or Mrs. Hawk! You're a real pal," he cried, waving his Stetson after it.

Totally caught up in Mother Nature's moment, he remembered reading about the 'Survival of the Fittest', in his science text. "So that's how it works," he marvelled, watching the hawk rise ever higher into the sky.

# ·⋆˚Chapter 11·⋆˚

When he strolled into the ranch office, Mom paid little attention to his arrival. She was busy preparing pay cheques for the cowboy crew. Picking a chair near the door, he plunked himself into it and waited for her to acknowledge him.

She finally looked up. Little Jake spoke first, hoping to divert her attention so she wouldn't ask too many prying questions.

"Gee, Mom, you should've seen the two hawks I spotted up near the Upper Meadows. One of them pulverized a crow. You shoulda' bin' there."

"Maybe, they've got a nest around there somewhere, Jake," she said, pleased with her son's sudden interest in the local bird life. "There you go. You see, there's always something interesting happening around the Ranch. That's why this is such a great place to be. Mother Nature is always at her best out here."

"Now that you're showing an interest in birds, maybe you'll help me with my 'Save the Burrowing Owls Project'. We have a few nests on the upper slopes of Wolverine Lake and we're hoping to make the owl colony much larger. What say? They're on the endangered species list, you know. I sure could use an extra hand."

"The last time we had a transplant, we actually had to dig out burrows by hand. You can help me find some old abandoned gopher holes for the half-dozen transplants coming in from Kamloops in the next few weeks."

"Sounds great, Mom! But can I do that later?"

"Why later, Jake? You like to get out on Kasey. Once

the owls have settled in and gotten used to their new home, they'll hopefully lay some eggs. You could ride over to check and make sure the eggs haven't been destroyed by skunks.

"Skunks! You said skunks! Come on, Mom! You can't be serious. You know how their stink makes me barf!"

Ignoring Little Jake's comment, Mom continued, "Would you like to start tomorrow?" She knew she was making him uncomfortable and enjoyed watching him squirm in his chair.

He knew he just had to use all of his time on his secret mission and his mom sure wasn't helping! "First it was a pesky crow and now it's a pesky mom wrecking all my plans," Little Jake mumbled and then stuttered, "I–I–I–I will, Mom, but later, okay? For the next while, I'd really like to go up to Billy Miner Lake to check on those hawks. If I find their nest, I'll be able to see if they've got chicks. Wouldn't that be great? There haven't been any of those big hawks around for the last few years, either."

"Oh, alright, but remember, you'd better be back before dark," she warned.

The next day, Little Jake could hardly wait to return to the Upper Meadows. It was a very long frustrating day because his school lessons took longer than usual. To make matters worse, Rock Creek asked him to clean and oil saddles and headstalls. Rock Creek was very fussy about horse gear. He knew he was expected to do the job right! And that meant hours of hard work. His arms and shoulders ached by the time he finished.

When he arrived at the cookhouse for a drink, he couldn't believe that the clock showed four p.m. Even though he was tired, he desperately wanted to go back to the snag!

In his wanderings around the Home Ranch, he hadn't

seen One-Eye anywhere. "Is he out cavorting with that coyote, again?" he pondered, as he took a quick glance around the ranch yard.

It wasn't suppertime yet but he managed to wheedle a bite to eat out of Sharon. He wolfed down the food, grabbed his Stetson and barrelled out of the cookhouse.

Hurrying back to the horse corral, he sped around the corner of the horsebarn, and skidded to a halt - sending gravel flying toward Kasey. She startled and jumped sideways into an old gelding who was trying to snitch some of her hay. She seemed to blame the old gelding for scaring her. With her ears flattened tightly against her head, she turned her hind end, ready to kick. The message was, "Keep your distance, Buster, or you'll be wearing a pair of horseshoes in your teeth!"

Little Jake watched and chuckled over the 'Horse Hopscotch' for a moment and then stepped into the corral hoping Kasey was over her snit. She kept flattening her ears even after her halter was on.

"I suppose now you're mad at me for taking you away from your feed and letting that gelding get it, eh, Kase? Just behave yourself! You'd better not buck me off, you hear," threatened Little Jake, as he swung into the saddle.

The April sun was getting low in the sky. With a cool breeze at their backs, Little Jake encouraged Kasey to stretch out into a easy lope. Kasey got over her anger quickly and moved along in a relaxed rhythm. A short distance before the snag, she came to a sliding stop right in the middle of a large bull wallow. A cloud of fine clay dust rose and settled over them, causing Little Jake to sputter and cough. Kasey had to snort to clear her nostrils, too.

While Little Jake continued to cough, Kasey gave a violent shake, covering both of them with a fine dust again. "Is this your way of paying me back for taking you away from that flake of hay?" he spat.

Pulling Kasey out of the wallow, he led her to a grove of aspens and tied her to a hung-up deadfall. "Humph, I wonder why she picked that wallow as a place to stop? Maybe she smelled something."

He slapped himself with his hat as he walked toward the snag. Dust still billowed from his jeans. He scanned uphill, downhill and along the horizon, but couldn't see anything that would have made her stop so suddenly.

Still puzzled, he decided the first thing he should do was to see if the roast bits were where he'd left them. "Hey, they're gone!" he said , not sure whether to be jubilant or upset.

Putting a dusty glove over his mouth, he reminded himself to be quiet. If by chance whatever took the scraps was still around, he didn't want to spook it!

"Wow! Look at all of these paw prints on the mound! And they go down the hole under the snag! "Some of them look like fresh dog tracks. I'll bet One-Eye was here! But I'm sure he wouldn't crawl down that dark hole! He could have eaten the meat, though. Yeah, that would be just like him," he grumbled, raising his arms in frustration.

"I'll have to put out some more scraps." Reaching into the front pocket of his jeans, Little Jake found it empty. His eyes widened as his hand darted from pocket to pocket, coming up empty. "I forgot the bait! How could I be so dumb!" he scolded himself.

Tripping over rocks and old branches, he careened down the slope toward Kasey. Snapping the lead off the deadfall, he grabbed the saddlehorn with both hands and vaulted into the saddle. By the time he found his seat, Kasey was already stretching out in a full gallop. She didn't need to be encouraged to go home. It was evident she intended to rescue her flake of hay.

Little Jake gave his mecate rein a lot of slack, determined to return with more scraps and get home before dark. ↑

# ˙⋆˙Chapter 12˙⋆˙

Kasey was heaving and covered in a lather by the time they pulled up at the back of the root cellar. Little Jake felt guilty for pushing her so hard. He knew if Grandpa or Rock Creek had seen her, they'd have been very upset with him.

He tied Kasey to some scrub willows growing out of the back of the root cellar - a spot where he was sure no one could see her.

Little Jake covered two steps at a time as he crashed up the cookhouse steps. Swinging around the screen door, he just about knocked his mom over. "Slow down, guy! What's the big panic? You'd think a grizzly bear was chewin' on your behind. Sharon told me that you'd already gobbled down your supper. How come you're back?"

"Guess I ate too fast, Mom. I'm still hungry," Little Jake said, thinking fast.

He slipped into an empty spot at the table. Rock Creek and the other buckaroos were busy filling their faces and paid little attention to his sudden appearance.

Grabbing a drumstick, he crammed it into his mouth hoping that with his mouth full, his mom wouldn't ask any further questions. It worked! She shook her head, stepped out the door and headed for the ranch office.

Leaving a good part of the meat on the bone, Little Jake glanced around to see if anyone was watching. He then slipped it into his jeans pocket.

Halfway through his second drumstick, Little Jake looked up and saw Rock Creek grinning at him. He choked, thinking he'd been caught red-handed!

"What's the matter, Little Buddy? That chicken still have feathers on 'er?" joked Rock Creek, grabbing another drumstick with his greasy fingers.

Little Jake's face flushed with embarrassment as he looked down at his plate, trying to avoid Rock Creek's stare. He looked up at Sharon and the rest of the buckaroos, out of the corner of his eye. He was relieved to see they weren't paying any attention, only Rock Creek was watching and grinning.

As he stuffed the third drumstick into his pocket, he caught Rock Creek's wink. Little Jake was convinced that Rock Creek knew he was up to something! He lifted his finger up to his lips just like Grampa used to. He hoped Rock Creek would keep his secret. Rock Creek winked again.

"I know! He's grinnin' because he probably got himself into a heap of trouble when he was my age. I'll bet he was no angel," Little Jake said, rolling his eyes.

With six half-eaten drumsticks in his pockets, he slid out from under the table and exited quickly so that no one would see his bulging pockets.

"That scalliwag's sure's actin' strange. I hope he isn't gettin' into some kind of trouble." said Sharon, shaking her head and glancing over at Rock Creek. Rock Creek just grinned a greasy toothless grin and winked at her.

Kasey had decided that day's riding was over. She had been digging herself quite a hole, showing Little Jake she was upset that he hadn't taken her over to rescue her flake of hay. Reluctant to go back to the Upper Meadows, she kept turning and pulling toward the corral. It was obvious she wanted to put a run on that old gelding.

"Smarten up, Kasey! I have to get back to the snag." Whoa! Whoa, now! Forget about your stupid hay! The gelding's finished it by now. Stand still, willya?" Little

Jake moved Kasey against the front wall of the root cellar and mounted.

He glanced over to the cookhouse wondering if he'd been spotted. Sure that no one was looking, he spurred Kasey into a fast trot. Just as they reached the aspens below the snag, she nearly dumped him.

Straddling her neck - he was hanging on for dear life! "Gee whiz, Kasey! That hurt!" Clutching a maneful of hair in a death grip, he used his other hand to push himself back over the saddlehorn. "Ouch! Ouch! I'll bet I came close to being the first ever - buckaroo missile! I don't know what's with you, Kasey? You've sure been makin' some weird stops lately. Warn me next time, willya!" he exclaimed.

He could feel Kasey's muscles tighten under him. Her foxy ears were pointed forward. Still smarting from his near tumble, he eased back into the saddle.

Straight ahead was a coyote intently watching the whole cowboy comedy. Relaxing his grip on the saddle-horn and mane, Little Jake sat stock still! The last thing he wanted to do was to scare it away.

He hoped Kasey wouldn't flinch. He felt her tremble under him. She began to shake her head and snort rollers*.

"Sh-h-h-h-h! Kasey," he said, trying to calm her.

Back legs tucked well under her, she shuffled backwards with quick steps. Eyes glued on the coyote, she spun around, and turned to face the coyote again. Little Jake was holding a tight rein to keep her from bolting! He knew that Kasey had seen many coyotes before, but that had been from a distance. This one was obviously 'too close for comfort'!

When Kasey was far enough back, she finally stopped trembling. Little Jake held his breath as he slowly stepped off her. He made sure the lead of his mecate was tucked under his belt. He didn't want a runaway!

Throughout Kasey's Upper Meadows line dance, the coyote sat on his haunches, twisting his head back and forth, studying his visitors with great interest.

The coyote stood up but did not leave. Little Jake took a few steps forward and the coyote darted behind the old pine tree. "Shucks! What'll I do now?" he said in disappointment. "I'll throw a drumstick over there, maybe he'll come back."

The wary coyote was partially hidden by the thick roots of the snag. His beady eyes and sharp nose were all that Little Jake could see. "He's not run very far. Could this be where he lives? Maybe he's got a food cache down that hole and is trying to protect it. I guess I'd better be careful," he cautioned himself, stepping away, not taking his eyes off the coyote.

If he had to beat a hasty retreat, he wanted to make sure he could see Kasey. Stepping back again, his boot heel caught a forked branch and he tripped. Arms flailing, he hit the ground with a thud!

His hat went cartwheeling down the hill. He was rolling over so it would be easier to stand up when he was startled by a streak of silver-grey flashing past his head. Instinctively, he lifted his elbow to protect himself!

Nothing happened! "Yowzers! That was close! I guess I scared him off for good that time," he gasped. The coyote was nowhere to be seen. Little Jake dug into his front pockets and wrenched out some more drumsticks. "I might as well get rid of these greasy things," he said, walking over and dropping them on the clay mound.

He was having second thoughts about a coyote ever being friendly. He bent down and searched for a stick in case the streak of silver came at him again. Picking up a thick pine branch, he tucked it under his arm. Straightening up, he took a quick glance at the mound.

"There he is!" cried Little Jake, tightly squeezing the pine branch under his arm. He was going to be ready this time. The coyote watched him vigilantly. "Yup! I think I'm right! He's probably upset because this is his home, otherwise he wouldn't still be 'hanging around'."

Little Jake giggled nervously as the coyote cocked his head from side to side. It was as if he was saying, "Now, why is this human being bothering me, anyway?"

The coyote stretched out on his belly and began to drag himself towards the mound.

"Maybe I should try talking to him. But, he'll need a name. Hmmm, let's see. What would be a good name?

Hmmm, coy-o-tee. Ki....o....tee! Ki-o-tee! Ki! Ki! That's it! I'll only use the first part. Ki, for short! Right on!"

"Here Ki! Come on, boy! Here, Ki!" repeated Little Jake, at the same time extending his hand out in friendship. He was amazed that he was close enough for him to admire his fuzzy, silvery coat. It looked so soft that he wished he could reach out and pet him.

Little Jake knew that most animals have an inbred instinct for safety - a place where they feel secure. Grandpa had told him about it when they were out catching horses one day.

"They like to keep a distance away from anything they think might threaten them. They need room to escape. If someone or something enters their zone of comfort, they become agitated, anxious and very unpredictable. That could become an unsafe situation. Until you build up complete trust with an animal, enter their personal space slowly and carefully."

Daylight was fading but Little Jake couldn't tear himself away from the exciting experience with Ki. "If I'm patient, maybe he'll come a little closer," he hoped, crouching down on one knee.

He decided to make himself appear smaller and less threatening. So he got down on both knees and slid backwards a few feet to ensure he wasn't intruding on the coyote's personal space. A sharp stone caught his left knee making him wince in pain.

Just as he lifted his knee to remove the stone, Ki streaked to the mound and grabbed the drumsticks. He was fast! So fast, that by the time Little Jake flung the stone aside, Ki had already disappeared down the hole at the base of the snag. "Boy, just like Wiley Coyote! I've never seen such a fast-movin' critter before! He'd make one —— cowdog!"

Feeling guilty about saying a swear word, he glanced over his shoulder half-expecting to see Mom standing there. He knew she didn't like anyone swearing and that included those roughshod buckaroos. She especially didn't like Little Jake spending too much time around the horse barn. "Where the air is always blue," she'd say.

Rock Creek happened to be one of the worst. Little Jake got quite a chuckle out of seeing Rock Creek being scolded by Mom. He'd just stand there with a snoose-loaded grin on his face and within moments forget himself and do it all over again.

"Mom, sure is strict about certain things," he chuckled, feeling silly about expecting to find her there. ⚘

# ⁺⁺⁺Chapter 13⁺⁺⁺

Waiting for Ki to reappear, Little Jake pulled up his pantleg to check on his sore knee. It had bled. "Oooo, that smarts!" "Where's that dumb rock, anyway?" Finding it, he kicked at it. It rolled only a few inches. Frustrated, he picked it up and without looking, hurled it as hard as he could, straining his arm and pulling his shoulder. "Great! Now everything hurts!

The rock went bouncing toward Kasey. It landed with a thump - waking her. Being only ground-tied, she spun around and headed for home. Little Jake limped after her, hollering for her to stop, but it was no use. No matter how much he called, Kasey wouldn't stop. "That stupid rock anyway!"

Muttering about his stupidity, Little Jake struggled over the hills and through the meadows towards the Home Ranch. It was getting dark fast. He felt sore all over. Not only did his knee hurt, but his arm and shoulder throbbed. Twisting his ankle, he whined, "These boots with undershot* heels, sure ain't made for walkin'!"

Much, much later, he finally spotted the flickering lights of the Home Ranch. Between where he was and the lights, he could make out a faint four-legged silhouette. Kasey had run out her booger and had obviously discovered some feed. "That glutton! A patch of young alfalfa is more important than I am. Now that's what I call a friend!" he exclaimed.

The darker it became, the spookier it became. Little Jake kept glancing over his shoulder, imagining wild animals were about to pounce on him. His imagination was really working overtime!

But soon, his biggest worry took over. "I hope Mom isn't sending out a search party!"

He was so tired and sore when he reached Kasey, he didn't have the energy to scold her. With the torn lead in his hand, he "ouched" himself into the saddle pulling his feet out of the stirrups to relieve the pressure. Kasey was so busy chomping alfalfa shoots, she didn't even react to him getting on.

She refused to budge when he squeezed her sides. Instead, she laid her ears back trying to intimidate Little Jake into letting her eat. It was obvious that her priority was to stay in 'Alfalfa Heaven'.

"If you don't git movin', horse, I'm gonna make coyote bait out of you!" he hollered. It was as if she knew exactly what Little Jake meant. She jumped forward and trotted for home, making Little Jake flinch with each bounce.

Rock Creek was strapping on his chinks when Little Jake eased himself through the horsebarn doorway, dragging his saddle behind him. "Hey, young fellah! Your mom's gettin' mighty anxious about your whereabouts. I was just about to saddle up and ride out to look for yuh! You'd better get that keester* of yourn' into the ranchhouse, pronto! She's madder than a hen that's lost her chicks to a mangy coyote!" he said, gruffly.

"Gee, I'm sorry 'bout all the trouble, Rock Creek! That stupid mare of mine ran off without me and I had to walk. I'll head soon's I turn her out."

"Never mind her. I'll do that. You'd better scoot your booties over there right now, young man!" he warned again, unbuckling his chinks.

Little Jake knew this meant trouble! If Mom had called Rock Creek out of the bunkhouse to go searching for him, she'd be fuming! "She'll be asking a lot of questions. I'd better come up with some good answers. I can't tell her the real reason why I was late just yet. If she finds out, she might never let me go out in the evening again," he gulped.

"I know, I'll blame it all on Kasey. After all she was the one that left me stranded! A-a-a-a-nd I can even show her the torn lead— that'll prove that Kasey ran off." Little Jake felt much better now that he thought he had an alibi.

All the lights were out at the ranchhouse except for the porch light. Little Jake hoped that Mom was already asleep and wouldn't badger him with questions. He took a deep breath and slipped ever so quietly into the ranchhouse.

His hopes were dashed! The silence was jarred by Mom's voice. "Jake, is that you? Why are you so late? Jake, are you alright?" she questioned, stopping him as he was opening the door of his bedroom.

"Yes, Mom. I'm fine. Sorry for being late but Kasey ran off and I had to walk home. Boy, are my feet ever sore!" he explained, hoping to gain some sympathy.

"Did she buck you off? You're not hurt are you?"

"I'm okay, Mom, honest!" Little Jake winced, feeling a twinge in his left foot. He wasn't lying! His body surely did ache!

"You'd better hit your bunk, Bucko! If you come in late like this again, you'll be grounded until you're old enough to shave. Remember that, Charlie!" Mom always called Little Jake; Charlie, when she was annoyed with him.

He rolled into bed slowly, trying not to press on any sore spots. He was relieved to finally be curled up under Old Smelly. Waiting for his aches to subside, sleep didn't come easy. All sorts of plans and ideas swirled around in his head. He finally drifted off, happy that he had completed the first phase of his secret mission.

# Chapter 14

The ranch rooster's raspy cock-a-doodle-doo jolted Little Jake out of a nightmare. "If you ever want to be a buckaroo, you'll have to have a cowdog!" He wasn't quite sure whose voice it was but he thought it might have been Gramps. He lay still for a moment trying to remember most of the dream, but the rooster's incessant crowing kept interrupting!

"I"ll just have to prove to Mom that I'm ready to have my own cowdog - that's all there is to it! I know I can be responsible - although after last night she might not think so. I'll make sure my chores are done every day from now on. That should convince her."

Still sore, he inched out of his bunk. He got dressed slowly and carefully trying to reduce the pain as much as possible.

"Ouch, that knee still hurts! I'll have to get Sharon to look at it when I go for breakfast. I guess I'd better put on my sneakers to do my chores. My toes still feel like Kasey stepped all over them," he said, stumbling off like an old stove-up cowboy.

He made sure he was on his best behaviour. After breakfast, he offered to help Mom with jobs around the office. Little Jake fed the chickens, the cats, dogs and the horses the buckaroos weren't using that day. Then he returned to the ranch office and spent time eagerly doing school lessons, trying to impress his mom.

He was the only kid at the Ranch and oftentimes felt quite alone. Sometimes, he wished he was back at the Coast where he could share his adventures with his city pals. At the Ranch, much of his spare time was spent with grown-ups.

As the day wore on, he found it more and more difficult to concentrate on his 'home schooling'. The longer he sat in his old desk, the more twitchy he became. Finally finished, he rushed out of the office door- he knew exactly where he was going!

"I'll bet Ki's waiting for us, Kase. He sure loves those meat scraps. I'll bet he's hoping his groceries will get delivered pretty quick. And I'll even bet you a bucket of oats that he'll be there waiting." He paused like he expected Kasey to respond. All she did was flick her ears back and forth.

They fast-trotted and loped all the way, both enjoying the ride. "There he is, Kase! Just like I said."

Ki was more accepting of Little Jake's presence today. Although he insisted on keeping his distance, he didn't run off. That pleased Little Jake immensely! "Maybe some day you'll take scraps right out of my hand, eh, Ki? Wouldn't that be something to tell everyone."

Deep down, Little Jake knew that taming a wild creature might be impossible. However, he hoped if he was patient, he might be lucky. It was times like these, that Little Jake felt Grandpa's presence. "Yup, I'll bet he's sitting on that old snag right now, grinning away at what I'm trying to do."

Several days passed and Little Jake continued his trips to the old pine snag. As he rode up, he noticed Ki wagging his bushy tail. This hadn't happened before.

Sitting cross-legged, a few feet below the den, Little Jake tried to coax Ki to come closer. For some reason, Ki's tail was wagging like crazy! His head was cocked and he seemed to be looking over Little Jake's shoulder. "That's odd! What's making him do that?" wondered Little Jake.

Thinking there might be something behind him, Little Jake turned to look. Swoosh! Something brushed by his right shoulder - startling him! Rolling out of the way, he realized that the 'swoosh' was none other than One-Eye. Annoyed, Little Jake scolded him. "Cheesh, One-Eye, You'll scare Ki away! You'll wreck all my hard work!"

Just as he finished scolding, Ki ran at One-Eye! Dumbfounded, Little Jake anticipated a fight. He immediately tensed up not knowing what to do. One thing he did know was that One-Eye was too old to be fighting! Little Jake's first impulse was to assist One-Eye. In a panic, he searched the hillside for something to ward off the coyote.

A knotted pine branch in his hand, he rushed toward the inter-locked fur ball. Standing straddle-legged, an arms length from the growling mass of fur, Little Jake raised the stick waiting for his opportunity to strike Ki!

"Arr-arr-arr," they growled, as they tumbled and rolled down the hill. Little Jake scrambled after them. Every time he lifted his stick, the fur ball zagged and then zigged. He just couldn't land a blow, afraid that he might strike One-Eye.

They continued to roll down the hill towards Kasey. Wild-eyed, she tried to jump aside but they rolled right under her belly, making her snort and prance. It was lucky for Little Jake that he'd tied Kasey securely this time, otherwise he'd have had another sore-footed stroll home.

Holding the branch over his shoulder, he gave up on trying to use it. Instead he started hollering and screaming. It worked! They parted and skittered off in opposite directions. Little Jake was relieved and looked for signs of blood in the grass. There were none, only small hunks of hair.

He was now standing between One-Eye and Ki. Their tails were tucked between their legs and they were both crouched down and staring at each other. Spinning around simultaneously, they faced one another again. Their heads were low to the ground, haunches in the air, tails wagging. Little Jake was perplexed!

"Wagging tails? Only friends would wag their tails! Whats' going on?" shouted Little Jake. "You dumb, dumbs! You scared the living daylights out of me! That wasn't a fight. You were just horsing around, weren't you?" he said, feeling relieved. "You were just playing a game, right?"

He recalled seeing ranch cowdogs do the exact same thing. A dog would dart away in a flurry and the other one would take up the chase. With their tails tucked, they'd zig and zag, doing all sorts of feinting maneuvers. It was very comical to watch. "What a relief!" sighed Little Jake, flipping off his Stetson and wiping his brow.

Still confused, he slumped onto the bunchgrass. "So it was you two playing canine tag that moonlit night near the horse corrals. Humdinger! this means you're buddies!" Little Jake beamed, as he tossed his hat up into the air.

Propping himself up on his elbow, he watched as One-Eye and Ki chased each other around. They continued to feint and charge until their tongues were lolling out. After flattening out a large area of grass, they finally tired and stretched out on their bellies. They totally ignored Little Jake.

After a short rest, their bodies still heaving, they took off circling the snag at a dead run. Leaping over the snag, they just missed landing on Little Jake. Using him as a shield, they came to a screeching halt on either side of him and prepared to mount another attack.

Ki had let down his guard as his full attention was on One-Eye. Little Jake sat very still. If he reached out, he'd be able to touch Ki! Yet, he didn't dare! He knew if it was to happen, Ki would have to come to him.

"I'll bet they've played this game many times. Just look at them. They're stretched out - shoulder to shoulder, like they've been best pals for years. I shure wish I had a camera."

"Are you two grinning at me? That was some trick you pulled on me - you rascals!" Little Jake was overcome with so much joy and relief, he broke into a fit of giggles. He rolled in the grass and slapped at the ground. One-Eye and Ki got up on their haunches and twisted their heads from side to side, confused by his erratic behaviour.

Little Jake couldn't resist feigning a lunge at the two canines. Spooked, they scattered in different directions, with their tails tucked between their legs. Again, Little Jake roared with laughter. "You guys look like you've just seen a ghost!" he giggled some more.

As he was wiping his brow with his sleeve, he was bowled over by One-Eye. "One-Eye! What was that for? It's too warm, I don't want to tussle right now."

When One-Eye rushed Little Jake, Ki scooted behind the snag.

"Now look what you've done, One-Eye!" Little Jake said, angrily. Knowing by the tone of his voice that he was upset with him, One-Eye cowered and slunk away.

Little Jake coaxed him to come back. "Oh, come here, you old galoot. I know you didn't mean to scare Ki away."

One-Eye slowly inched over and put his front paws across Little Jake's lap. Rolling his eyes upward and wagging his tail, he showed Little Jake that he accepted his apology.

Little Jake placed his hand on One-Eye's head and stroked it. One-Eye let out a big sigh. "How long have you and Ki been pals, Old Timer?"

He thought about the time Rock Creek and Grandpa discussed coyotes following cow herds during turnouts and roundups. This got Little Jake to thinking. I wonder if one of the coyotes might have been Ki? Maybe he'd been following and watching the cowdogs and learned to imitate their moves. It could have been One-Eye that he was watching. His mind began to fill with all sorts of possibilities.

"I guess there's only one way to find out," he decided. "I'll try some cowdog signals and see what happens." Standing up, Little Jake moved a short distance downhill and called, "Come!" One-Eye responded immediately and rushed over to Little Jake. Ki reacted too, but stopped short, keeping One-Eye between himself and Little Jake. "Hmmm, Ki paid attention. But he probably moved because One-Eye did. But then it's possible that he understood the signal. Oh, well. I guess time will tell," he shrugged.

"You know, Ki. If you actually understand some commands, you could be the very first cow coyote in the world. What do you say about that?" Ki only reacted by cocking his head to one side.

"A cow coyote...yeppasiree! Now wouldn't that be something! But cow coyote is too hard to say. Let's see 'cow-ote' or maybe it should be 'cowyote' Hey, I like that! A 'cowyote' Do you like that, Ki?" asked Little Jake, as if he expected Ki to reply, "Yeppasiree!"

Little Jake stretched out his arm and said, "I dub thee, Ki the 'cowyote'. That makes it official. Okay, Ki? And now, you'll have to make sure you learn all the cowdog commands, you hear!" Ki stretched out his neck and let out a sharp yip. "I knew you could say, "Yeppasiree," giggled Little Jake.

# ·⋆˙Chapter 15·⋆·˙

One-Eye pawed at Little Jake's leg to get his attention. He was anticipating another command. Sitting a safe distance away, Ki paid close attention, watching One-Eye's and Little Jake's every move.

Little Jake wanted to start with something simple. He groped through the bunchgrass looking for a small dry limb to toss. Finding a short, thin one, he flung it downhill. Both One-Eye and Ki raced to grab it.

On the next throw, it was Ki that ended up with the stick in his teeth. He was younger and faster than the aging One-Eye. Carrying the limb back part ways, he dropped it for One-Eye, seemingly saying, " Here, you take it over to Little Jake."

"Holy cow! If Ki knows everything One-Eye knows, he'll turn out to be one terrific cowyote!" concluded Little Jake.

Little Jake decided that he'd have to bring One-Eye along from now on, to help with Ki's training. "Humdinger! I will be the only one in the whole wide world to have a 'cowyote'!" he bragged to himself. "I bet that'll impress those buckaroos!"

One-Eye picked up the twig and dropped it on Little Jake's toe and waited for another toss. Instead he bent down and gave him a big hug. "If it wasn't for you, One-Eye, this never would have happened!"

Accepting the compliment, One-Eye planted a slurpy kiss across Little Jake's mouth. "Yuckers!" he sputtered, wiping off the slobber. "One-Eye, you must be the world's 'kissingest' cowdog! Yuck! Yuck! Yuck!"

It was time to leave. Bubbling with excitement, Little

Jake skipped down the slope toward Kasey.

Kasey had pulled on the lead until she'd cracked the aspen branch. It only held by a sliver of bark as she stretched to reach more grass. "The grass is always greener somewhere else, isn't it, Kase?" With that said, Kasey looked up at Little Jake and quit filling her belly.

Little Jake pushed up on the saddlehorn to straighten out the saddle. As he recinched, One-Eye stood nearby and whimpered. Just as Little Jake reached to turn the stirrup for his boot, One-Eye stood up on his hind legs and placed his front paws on the fender* of the saddle.

"What's this all about, One-Eye? Are you asking for a lift? Well, old-timer. It's not very often a cowdog rides a cowpony but I guess you've decided today's the day. It seems you're going to become a hitch-hiker in your old age. You must be really tuckered out. Come here and I'll hoist you up. Kasey, you stand still now. Whoa! I know you're not used to hauling double, especially dogs, but let's do it anyway."

Kasey seemed to understand and stood perfectly still. With One-Eye draped over the seat of the saddle, Little Jake slipped in behind the cantle clutching onto to One-Eye's coat with one hand and picking up the mecate rein with the other.

He eased Kasey into a walk, trying to make all three of them as comfortable as possible. Kasey was anxious to get back and kept trying to trot making it very uncomfortable for One-Eye. He whimpered with each bounce. Little Jake kept trying to ease Kasey back into a walk. He felt like whimpering too. Sitting behind the cantle with his feet out of the stirrups really hurt his bum.

With his hand resting on One-Eye's glossy black coat, he kept thinking about what an exceptional cowdog One-Eye was, at the same time saddened by One-Eye's old age.

He was fifteen years old - that made him one hundred and five in human years. "I hope you're going to be around for a while yet, old fellah! You know, you're my best pal now that I don't have Gramps around anymore." 🌿

# ⋆₊⋆Chapter 16⋆₊⋆

Days passed on and Little Jake found it more and more difficult to concentrate on school lessons and chores. He mind was consumed with winning Ki's trust and training him to be his 'secret cowdog'. With all the trips they'd made to the snag, One-Eye anticipated Little Jake's every move. That was what he lived for. He not only enjoyed being with Little Jake but he still loved travelling out on the range. Whenever they left for the snag, Little Jake held Kasey back so that One-Eye could keep up.

Ki had become very predictable. Whenever they arrived, he was sitting on the mound at the base of the snag. He was always particularly pleased to see One-Eye. Crouching down, he'd feign an attack on One-Eye hoping he would return the charge. But the game of charge got shorter after each visit. One-Eye's trip to the snag was tuckering him out. He mostly wanted to rest when he got there.

Sometimes he'd oblige Ki with a short romp. Then Ki would return to his mound and wait for Little Jake to produce the expected tidbits. Little Jake hoped Ki wasn't becoming too accustomed to this unnatural food supply.

Grandpa had cautioned him about feeding human food to wild creatures. Ki's main foods were mice, gophers, rabbits, squirrels and other small animals. When Ki hunted, he helped to keep the populations of these creatures in balance. But at the same, time, he knew that the scraps helped to establish trust and friendship with Ki. "Oh, well," he rationalized, "we'll pretend the scraps are only dessert."

While Ki and One-Eye shared the cookhouse scraps, Little Jake stretched out in the bunchgrass and stared at the puffy clouds in the deep blue sky. Within moments, he spotted one of the hawks doing spirals above Billy Miner Lake. Even though it was quite some distance away, it was beautiful to watch.

The hawk's silvery wings reflected the sunlight as it changed the tilt of its flight patterns. Other than an occasional shriek, it was very serene. "I wonder if one of those hawks isn't Gramps watching over us." mused Little Jake, for a moment wishing he could float in the sky, like the hawk.

"Well, that's enough lazin' around, One-Eye. I guess we'd better get to it. Okay, you two. Pay attention! Let's try some commands," he continued, putting One-Eye through the paces.

They had worked very hard. He hoped Ki would mimic every move One-Eye made. He wasn't disappointed, he was ecstatic! He shortened his visit this day because he was so pleased with both their responses.

The next day was a hot, muggy May day. Little Jake's energy was spent by the time they reached the snag. He searched around for some shade and stretched out against a wide tall stump.

A drooping One-Eye sidled over and crawled up onto his lap. He was perplexed by One-Eye's insistence about being on his lap. He had never done this before. "It's too hot, One-Eye," cried Little Jake, trying to push him off. One-Eye resisted and stayed on Little Jake's lap. "Right now, I don't have the energy to battle with you, dog. So stay if you must," grumbled Little Jake, dropping his arms to the ground.

One-Eye turned his head upward and leaned tightly against Little Jake's chest making him even hotter. He stared up into Little Jake's eyes and whined as if he had something very important to tell him.

A cool breeze slipped down through the aspens and washed over Little Jake's sweaty face. "Ahhhh! That feels good!" he exclaimed. Deciding not to disturb One-Eye, he let his body go limp and enjoyed the special moment with his old friend.

The last time Little Jake had looked, Ki had been grabbing a coyote nap in the shade of the snag. He startled when Little Jake suddenly stretched and tried to shake the numbness out of his leg. Although he was in the shade, the warm air caused Little Jake to doze off.

Something warm and wet touched his hand. Thinking it might be a snake, he leaped up dumping One-Eye. He looked at where his hand had been. There wasn't anything there! It hadn't been One-Eye because his head was facing the other way.

He leaned against the stump, and continued to survey the grass for any sign of a snake. Nothing wiggled through the grass. "There's nothing here!"

Turning to look at the snag, he realized Ki wasn't there. Instead he was behind the stump. "Ki, did you lick my hand, you rascal? Little Jake lifted his hand for a closer look. Putting his hand up to his nose, he could smell the cookhouse leftovers on his fingers. "Uh, huh! So that's what happened! You smelled the meat on my fingers and licked them, right, Ki?"

"I guess when I yanked my hand back, I must have scared you off. I wrecked it!" he complained, disgusted with himself. "It will probably be ages before I can get you to come that close again." ∩

# ·₊*Chapter 17·₊*

The breeze had died down and it had become exceptionally muggy. Sweat dribbled down Little Jake's back making his shirt feel clammy.

A canopy of thick black clouds moved towards them from the west. The cold blast of air signaled an approaching thunderstorm. Little Jake knew that this could mean trouble! He hadn't brought his slicker. "We'd better hightail it out of here before we get drenched," he said - panic showing in his voice.

The first clap of thunder sent Ki scurrying down the hole into his den. Little Jake hobbled off toward Kasey as fast as his numb leg would carry him. Trembling from the thunder, Kasey anxiously pounded the ground with her hoof.

It was dangerous to be out in the open during a thunder and lightning storm. His leg felt better by the time he reached Kasey. He yanked up on the cinch making it extra tight, causing Kasey to suck in air and hump up. Fumbling to untie the lead, he didn't notice the end of it drop out from under his belt. He stepped on it making Kasey pull back and rear. Falling backwards his foot got hung-up in the stirrup!

Hitting the ground, he grabbed for the lead, giving himself a nasty rope burn as it slid through his fingers. He managed to hold onto Kasey. He shuddered, thinking about what could have happened if Kasey had panicked and he'd been dragged.

Kasey took a step backward and that released Little Jake's foot. Holding the lead in both hands, he gathered himself for a moment-pulled himself up and then swung into the saddle. Little Jake made sure the lead was tucked securely under his belt. "Boy, that was too close for comfort!" he solemnly stated, as he took off his Stetson and wiped his brow.

They had only gone a short distance before he realized that One-Eye wasn't following. Spinning Kasey around, they trotted back towards the snag. One-Eye sat near the tall stump as if he'd been tied to it. His tongue was hanging out and he didn't look like he planned to move. The heat and humidity had sapped the old dog's energy. All he seemed to want to do was lie there and sleep.

"Hey, old man, I suppose you expect Kasey to be your taxi again." Once again, Little Jake made sure the lead was tightly tucked under his belt as he stepped off Kasey. There was no way that he wanted to walk home in a thunderstorm.

This time, he'd be ready if a clap of thunder boogered Kasey. Both his hands were now free to load One-Eye. He put a hand on One-Eye's collar and wrapped his other arm around his belly. One-Eye squirmed and swam as Little Jake struggled to lift him into the saddle.

He praised Kasey for showing patience at a time like this. Kasey didn't start dancing around until more thunder rolled in the distance. However after a third try to hoist One-Eye onto her back, she started to lose patience. As was her habit, she began to pound the ground with her hoof.

A crash of thunder, directly overhead, shook the ground around them causing her to rear and unload One-Eye right on top of Little Jake. Hurrying to push One-Eye off, he snatched the leather popper, at the end of the lead, just in time. This time Kasey dragged Little Jake along for a few feet before he bounded up and was able to dig in his heels to hold and try to calm her. "Whoa, girl! Whoa, now," soothed Little Jake.

Kasey reared twice more; her eyes rolling as lightning struck a tree on the edge of the Upper Meadows. She came down with a thud, just missing his foot. He gave her a little more slack and she began to settle down. "Whoa! Kasey, Whoa Now!" She continued to side-step around Little Jake, just missing One-Eye. He cowered and tried to hide behind Little Jake. Tripping over One-Eye, Little Jake hung onto the mecate lead to keep his balance.

He knew he needed to relax if he expected Kasey to do the same. He let some of the lead slip through his hands to take the pressure off Kasey's head. It helped! "Easy, girl, easy," he said, giving her even more slack.

A double-forked bolt of lightning followed by sheet lightning lit up the whole upper valley. Large droplets of rain began to pelt down. It was such a torrent that the huge droplets felt like hail. "I've got to find cover! It's too late to make a dash for home!" cried Little Jake, pulling Kasey toward nearby trees.

A massive black cloud let loose. He stopped short, remembering a T.V. weatherman talking about storms. "If ever you're caught in a lightning storm, look for a low spot and stay away from trees." He spun Kasey around and searched the meadows for the nearest low spot.

"Yeah, The bull wallow, over there. Come on, Kasey!" demanded Little Jake. Already thoroughly drenched, he was no longer concerned about keeping dry. He was only concerned with the lightning striking so often and so close.

Kasey balked as Little Jake tried to move her away from the trees. She kept turning trying to get under a tall fir tree. "Kasey, you don't want to go there! That tree is the biggest lightning rod out here! Now, come on! This is no time to be stubborn!" he scolded, water dripping into his eyes.

One-Eye understood what Little Jake wanted and got behind Kasey and snapped at her heels. She put her ears back and struck out at One-Eye. One-Eye anticipated the next flying hoof and made sure he jumped back in the nick of time. One more bark from One-Eye and Kasey trotted alongside Little Jake towards the bull wallow.

More thunder jolted them just as they slid over the rim of the wallow. Mammoth-sized raindrops continued to pound them. Crouching down as low as possible, they prepared to wait out the storm.

Kasey had been taught to lie down when she was first trained as a young filly. With Little Jake's coaxing, she remembered the trick. Buckling her back legs slightly, she folded forward and plunked herself down in the muddy wallow. Little Jake squeezed in between the upper edge of the wallow and Kasey. One-Eye scampered over the top of Kasey and tucked his head under Little Jake's arm.

Lightning crashed and thunder continued to rumble! The lightning kept lighting everything around them. One strike hit just above the wallow. Little Jake could feel his hair and One-Eye's coat flare out from all of the electricity in the air. Kasey shook! Everytime the lightning crackled, One-Eye pushed his head further under Little Jake's arm.

Kasey kept shaking her head to get rid of the rainwater. With torrents of water cascading off his soggy Stetson, Little Jake poked up at the sodden brim and peeked over the edge of the wallow.

He hoped to see the black clouds moving away. What he saw was a standing dead aspen smouldering just a few feet from the big fir tree where Kasey had wanted to take refuge. The heavy rain had put the flames out but wisps of smoke continued to lift into the darkened sky! "Holy smoke!" gasped Little Jake, "that was too close for comfort."

Amazingly, Kasey held her spot throughout the rest of the storm. Even a cowdog resting against her rump, didn't seem to faze her. "I'm sure glad you remembered how to lie down and stay down until I said it was okay to get up, Kase! You're a good horse," said Little Jake giving her a pat on the neck.

Strong winds whipped up, causing the storm to move off to the east. Little Jake crawled up onto the upper bank of the wallow. Kasey and One-Eye immediately followed creating a miniature mud slide.

Once up on the grass, both Kasey and One-Eye gave a violent shake drenching Little Jake even more. "And that's what I get for saving your hides?" he muttered, using his sodden wild rag* to wipe the mud off his face.

Trying to wring out his hat - he totally wrecked its shape. Squishing his way over to Kasey, he leaned against her and emptied his mud-filled boots. "You know what, One-Eye? Not only do I have a ten gallon hat, but now I've got ten gallon boots," he chuckled half-heartedly, as he poured a mixture of mud and water out of each one.

One-Eye gave one more full-body shake and then nudged Little Jake with his snout. "What is it, One-Eye? What are you doing that for?" he asked, still trying to squeeze rainwater out of his clothes. He peeled his shirt off and had it twisted into a tight rope. He whipped out the mud-covered rag with both hands and eased it onto his back. "Wooooo....!" That's cold!" he quivered.

Meanwhile One-Eye was standing with his front paws on the fender of the saddle again. "Oh, I know," groaned Little Jake, "you still want that ride home, don't you, you wet smelly thing!"

With thunder clapping in the distance, Little Jake hoisted and grunted, trying to get One-Eye onto the mud-caked saddle. One-Eye scratched deep gouges into the saddle leather as he clawed to get a grip. But he just kept sliding off. Little Jake finally got his shoulder under One-Eye's bum and got him on. Holding him by the scruff of his neck, so he wouldn't slip off, Little Jake settled himself behind the cantle of the saddle.

Squishing and squeeking, they did an awkward, uncomfortable lope back to the Home Ranch. Everytime Kasey's legs hit the ground, muddy water oozed between Little Jake's toes. It felt horrible! His Stetson looked like an upside down funnel and dripped continuously on top of One-Eye who re-paid Little Jake by shaking his wet head violently.

This just added extra discomfort to Little Jake's ride home. "Quit shaking, you smelly canine!" he complained, trying to anticipate One-Eye's next shake by shielding himself with his arm.

Much later, in total misery, they reached the horse barn. Little Jake hauled One-Eye out of the saddle and laid him down on a pile of loose hay covered by a gun-nysack. "There, old pal, that will make you comfortable for the night. You'll be dry before you know it. I'm sure you'll be feeling a lot better tomorrow."

Next off, was the muddy saddle. With the soggy weight off her back, Kasey shook her whole body and gave Little Jake a final drenching 'for good measure'. "Jumpin' jelly beans, gal! I really needed that!" he sput-tered, spitting out bits of mud. He shivered as he gave Kasey a quick rub down.

Little Jake pulled the barn door closed and sloshed his way into the ranch house for a hot bath. He was beat, very cold and still very wet. The hot bath got rid of the shivers and made him sleepy. It was early to bed that night. He didn't even bother with supper.

Another storm moved in that night. The thunder, lightning and heavy rain created quite a spectacle over the Nicola Valley but Little Jake slept like a log.

He awoke very early the next morning, thinking about his pal, One-Eye. "I hope, he's had a good rest and he's feeling better this morning."

# ⋆⋆*Chapter 18*⋆⋆

It was Saturday, his favourite day of the week mostly because there wouldn't be any school work. Even though he was wide awake, it felt especially cosy under Old Smelly. "Hmmm, maybe I should have another wee nap." He was about to finish with, "I think that's a great idea!" When, someone rattled his bedroom door .

"Hey, you lazy saddle bum, are you up yet? We're movin' some steers up past Raven Lake. Wanna join up? Better get a saddle on!" The voice was Rock Creek's.

Little Jake was torn. He really wanted to go on the 'Drive'* but his secret mission with One-Eye and Ki was more important right now. He knew he'd probably lose favour with Rock Creek by not going, but his desire to be out at the snag was just too strong.

"I'm not going, Rock Creek!" he shouted back.

"What's the problem, buckaroo? You feelin' under the weather?"

"Nope, I have something else I've got to do today!" he replied, pulling Old Smelly over his head, hoping Rock Creek wouldn't come in.

"Yuh shure you're okay? You're not soundin' like yourself! What have yuh got to do that's more important than joinin' the crew? You're puzzlin' me, son. But suit yourself, we'll be leavin' in a half-hour."

Little Jake didn't respond this time. He was relieved to hear Rock Creek tromping down the stairs. Knowing that he'd be going over to tell his mom, his relief was short-lived. He was sure she would be coming over to see if he was okay.

His tummy started growling, reacting to the bacon and cinnamon bun smells wafting through his open bedroom window. "Boy, my gut sounds just like that thunder last night." he giggled.

The grumbling was causing gas to well up so he let out a long smelly fart. Fanning his comforter up and down, he tried to get rid of the smell. "Oooo-wheee! That's awful! Too bad Rock Creek hadn't waited," he smirked, bouncing around in his bed.

He just couldn't stop giggling, even after he got dressed and walked out on the ranch house porch. He punched at his Stetson trying to get its shape back. He plunked it on his head and looked into the window of the ranch house. Not only was it mis-shapen but it had shrunk. "Boy, doesn't that look just dandy! Shure wish I had that new silverbelly from Andy's," he scowled and then broke into giggles as he looked at his reflection one more time.

Opening the cookhouse door, he wondered why his mom hadn't been over to check on him. He expected there would be a bunch of questions. Surprisingly, she said nothing.

"This is not like Mom! She's always prying into everything I do. She's probably giving me the cold shoulder because I didn't go out with the crew," figured Little Jake. "Oh, well!"

Mom hadn't even looked up when he came into the cookhouse. She ate, put her dishes into the sink and walked out. Little Jake felt very uncomfortable when she ignored him like that.

Slurping a gob of strawberry jam off his thumb, he headed out. "I'd better get out and find One-Eye." Stuffing the last bit of raisin toast into his mouth, he jammed on his shrunken, deformed Stetson. Barrelling out onto the porch, he instinctively jumped off the top step to avoid tripping over One-Eye.

Even though One-Eye had been stepped on many times by the buckaroos, he insisted on sleeping on his favourite step. They had gotten used to doing a pirouette when they tromped out of the cookhouse in a hurry.

Landing in the dirt at the bottom of the stairs, Little Jake realized One-Eye wasn't there. One-Eye was always there in the morning!

Little Jake turned toward the horse barn and called and whistled. There was absolutely no sign of One-Eye. "Gosh, maybe he's still laid up in the barn. I'd better get over there and check."

Worried, he ran as fast as his legs would go. "He's not here and his bed's empty. He must be okay. I wonder if he headed up to the snag without me?"

He hurried over to Kasey's stall and was met with a nicker. He gave her a couple of quick swipes with a brush and said, "You loved being in here out of that storm, didn't you, Kase?" Reaching for her headstall, he slipped it on and lead her out of the barn.

Anxious to get to the snag, he jumped on bareback. Kasey seemed to sense Little Jake's urgency and eased into an immediate lope. She was well rested and they got there in record time. She didn't make any surprise stops, standing still as Little Jake dismounted.

Scanning the hillside near the snag, he didn't see any sign of One-Eye. The only thing moving in the early morning breeze was the bunchgrass and the quaking aspen leaves. Little Jake's heart dropped into his still soggy boots. There was absolutely no sign of One-Eye!

"Ki's not here either. Where could those rascals be?"

Turning to check out the nearby aspen grove, he spotted something move. His eyes glued to the spot. Kasey saw it too. She stood rigid - her ears pointing directly toward the trees.

"Ah! What a relief! It's Ki! I'll bet One-Eye's nearby," said Little Jake, feeling much better. Ki had something hanging out of his mouth. It looked like it might be a gopher. "Is that your breakfast, Ki?" shouted Little Jake. "Is One-Eye hunting for gophers, too?" he asked, hopefully.

Little Jake stuck two fingers into his mouth and whistled to see if One-Eye would respond. The whistle startled Ki causing him to drop his kill and disappear into the trees. "Darn! I didn't want that to happen!"

But within moments, Ki was back to pick up his breakfast. The gopher dangling out of both sides of his mouth, he stood statue still and stared back at Little Jake.

"Where's One-Eye? Have you seen, him?" implored Little Jake. As usual, Ki cocked his head, trying to figure out what Little Jake was asking. However, he did seem to react to One-Eye's name. He dropped the gopher and let out a quick sharp howl.

This time, Little Jake was startled and jumped back. "Come over here, Ki." Ki took a few steps towards him and dropped the gopher between them. He backed away and waited for Little Jake to make a move.

"Is this my breakfast, Ki? Thanks, but, no thanks! I've already had breakfast and I like my meat cooked," joked Little Jake. "Does this mean we're pals? You're trying to pay me back for all the scraps I've hauled over here, right?"

All that this one-sided conversation did was make Ki continue to cock his head from side to side. He seemed to be thinking long and hard about what Little Jake had said.

"Where is One-Eye, Ki?" Little Jake asked, one more

time. This time Ki lifted his snout and let out a louder and sharper howl, making Little Jake flinch.

A snapping branch spun Little Jake around. He hoped it was One-Eye. As Little Jake turned towards the sound, Ki darted down his den hole. It wasn't One-Eye. It was Kasey who broke the branch. They were the only ones out there. The dead gopher was gone too.

Discouraged, Little Jake walked back toward his cowpony, trying to decide on whether he should go home. As he reached to untie the lead, a yip interrupted his action. It was Ki sitting on the mound without the gopher. He was scanning the meadows and the aspen groves. "I wonder if he's still looking for One-Eye?"

He retied Kasey and walked back towards Ki, "Now don't go disappearin' on me again, you hear! You know, Ki, maybe One-Eye sneaked off to follow Rock Creek. I know he loves going on a 'Drive'. I'll bet that's where that rascal ended up."

"Well, what do we do now, Ki?" asked Little Jake.

An important decision had to be made. Should he spend time with Ki or search for One-Eye? Ki was willing to stay around. "Well, since I'm here and you seem to want to hang around, I'll see if you can work without One-Eye."

"Okay, buddy. Let's try a few commands and see what you can do." Little Jake put his whistle into his mouth and blew! Twisting his head from side to side, Ki didn't move. "Come on, Cowyote, you know what that whistle meant," coaxed Little Jake. He blew again. This time Ki responded immediately. He lay out flat and gave Little Jake his full attention.

The next command asked Ki to go to the right. He leapt up out of his prone position and ran in the exact direction he was supposed to go. "Wow! He's like a streak of lightning! Boy, he's good!" grinned Little Jake. "Those hotshot buckaroos are sure going to be in for a surprise! They'll soon find out who has the best cowdog, ....er, best 'cowyote' in the Nicola Valley," he gloated. His final call was, "That'll do!" Ki headed behind Little Jake and lay prone and panted away. He didn't get too close, making sure his personal safety zone was intact. "Well, Ki, not only are you fast, you're really smart." Ki had what looked like a grin across his snout. He seemed to be saying, "Yeppasiree, I'm pretty darn good, aren't I?"

Little Jake was so pleased with Ki that he desperately wanted to pet him as a way to thank him for being such a co-operative "cowyote". However, he just stood and enjoyed the moment! "I'm not giving up ,Ki. Someday you'll crawl up on my lap, like One-Eye did."

"I'd better head, Ki. I'm still worried about One-Eye's whereabouts. Tipping his hat, 'good-bye', Little Jake left for home.

"Maybe, One-Eye will be snoozing on his favourite step at the cookhouse," he mulled, as he rode home.

He thought about Grandpa's story of an old dog he once had. The old dog had wandered off into the hills to die. Gramps called it, "...to that Ranch across the Great Divide."

Little Jake swallowed hard thinking about such a possibility for One-Eye. A tear rolled off his cheek and spattered on the toe of his dusty boot. He wondered whether he would ever see his old pal again.

Back at the Home Ranch, Little Jake looked everywhere but couldn't find One-Eye.

The cowboy crew had returned, except for Skinny and Rolf who stayed at the Raven Lake cowcamp. Little Jake rushed over to see if One-Eye had returned with Rock Creek. He hadn't!

Fearing the worst, he burst into tears. Puzzled by Little Jake's behaviour, Rock Creek crouched down so he could look directly at him. "Whoa, little buddy, What's this all about?"

"Rock Creek," Little Jake sobbed, "I can't find One-Eye anywhere! He's not around! Do you think he left for the hills to die?"

Rock Creek stood up, wrapped his arm around him and turned his back to the crew. He had a feeling that Little Jake was right. For a moment, he was overcome, as he thought about not seeing his old cowdog ever again. He didn't want the crew to see the tear that rolled down his dust-encrusted face.

Clearing his throat, Rock Creek said, "It's okay, Son. One-Eye was a very special dog. And if he's gone, we'll both miss him an awful lot."

Seeing the muddy streak on Rock Creek's cheek made Little Jake feel better. This was the first time Little Jake had seen Rock Creek show his soft side. After all, One-Eye had been Rock Creek's working partner for many years.

"I'll bet he's gone across the Great Divide to 'that Ranch in the Sky'. He's probably running the range with your Grandpa," he said, trying to console Little Jake. Stepping back, he tapped Little Jake lightly on the shoulder, saying, "I'll be in the barn, if yuh need me, kid!"

That night, Little Jake went into see his mom before he went to bed. She reassured him that it was natural to grieve over lost friends.

"You know, son, sometimes some of your best friends happen to be animals. So, when you lose them, it's normal to feel sad," she said. Spending that time with his mom helped him deal with his grief.

Little Jake now spent much of his free time at the snag

with Ki. By putting his 'heart and soul' into his project, he felt he was honouring One-Eye.

For the longest time, whenever he arrived, Ki would crane his neck past Little Jake as if he still expected One-Eye to show up.

At first, they both had a difficult time concentrating on Ki's training. With time and with patience, Ki was able to follow the commands and work well without his mentor - One-Eye.

A few weeks after One-Eye had disappeared and Little Jake was sure he wouldn't be back, he put him to rest by saying a prayer, "One-Eye, I hope you and Gramps are looking out for each other up there! Thanks, One-Eye for being such a great pal and teaching Ki all the things a cowdog needs to know!" ✶

# ·*·Chapter 19·*·

The day had come to make his most important decision! "When should I introduce Ki to Mom and the buckaroos? Let's see, Mom will be going on 'Spring Turnout'* - yeah, that would be the time, alright - and the herd will pass right by the snag!

The special day turned out to be a beautiful sunny morning! This was the day that Rock Creek and the buckaroos would be moving cows and their calves to summer range. It would be a very early start and a long day.

Not wanting to leave familiar surroundings, the mother cows and calves would resist the push to summer pastures. Calves especially liked to go back to where they last suckled milk. Turning back 'herd quitters' would be the most difficult part of the 'Turnout'. The herd would slowly wend their way along, with their constant bawling echoing through the hills.

They would be spending their summer in the high country. Some of the buckaroos would stay in nearby cowcamps to make sure the herd stayed healthy. They'd also keep an eye out for predators, such as bears and cougars. The buckaroos would check water sources, pack in salt blocks and move the herd to make sure 'overgrazing'* didn't take place.

It was June and the first batch of about three hundred head of cows and calves were moving through the meadows and hills of the Double C Ranch. "Wow! Just like the drive in the movie, Lonesome Dove," thought Little Jake.

Even Mother Nature got dressed for the occasion. The

wild meadow flowers were in full bloom and large swallow-tail butterflies danced and skittered everywhere. They flitted around the horse's heads and under their bellies. One landed on Little Jake's gloved-hand which was resting on the saddlehorn. It hitched a ride for quite a distance. The swallow-tail just sat there and flitted its wings back and forth. Little Jake held his hand very still so that he could admire its beautiful colours. The butterfly finally fluttered away and landed on Kasey's head right between her ears. Thinking it was a horsefly, Kasey shook her head and scared the butterfly away. As it left, Little Jake called after it, "Hey, pretty butterfly! I hope you're my lucky charm!"

Robins, flickers, blackbirds, and whiskey jacks made a deafening chorus in the trees. A meadowlark sat on a fencepost and warbled out a beautiful melody. When the call of a loon drifted through the trees from a nearby lake, Little Jake, feeling giddy, tried to imitate its haunting call, making Kasey jump. He had to yank on the rein to check her to keep her from bumping into the herd. "It's okay, Kasey! There ain't a loon sitting on your back. At least not the bird kind," he joked.

Baby gophers and their vigilant parents stretched up beside hidden burrows to see what the commotion was all about. Spotting the cowdogs, they sent out a symphony of alarms and scampered down their holes. The cowdogs darted after them, from hole to hole - their chase squelched by buckaroos whistling and scolding.

The quiet creeks of winter, now flushed with snow melt, burbled over the rocks on their way to the many lakes in the Nicola Valley. Hot and thirsty, cows and calves veered off the trail to quench their thirst, interrupting the flow of the herd. The buckaroos had to be ever watchful to make sure the herd kept moving along. They didn't want any 'herd quitters' on their hands. If that happened, a lot of time would be wasted getting the herd headed in the right direction again.

This morning, in his excitement, Little Jake had forgotten to wash his face after breakfast. Trail dust clung to the sticky jam circling his mouth. From a distance, his face looked like a chicken with muddy feet had tracked across it.

Freddie was the first to notice Little Jake's unusual face decoration. "What yuh, grinnin' 'bout? How come you're wearin' lipstick this mornin'? Or is that one of those face tattoos?" he teased.

Turning red in the face, Little Jake swiped at his mouth with his sleeve. For a second, the sleeve stuck. As he pulled it away, fuzz from his shirt covered his mouth. Licking his lips, the fuzz stuck to his tongue.

"Yeck! Yeck!" he spat.

"With a mug like that, the only critter that would kiss yuh, would be a grizzly bear!" roared Freddie .

"Fun—ny!" Was all Little Jake muttered, as he plucked away at the fuzz on his tongue. "Wait till you see the surprise I've got in store for you, buckaroo! You won't be so fast to tease me," he whispered to himself.

While Little Jake spat, Freddie spurred his cowpony and trotted off to bring back a cow and calf heading for the trees. "Good riddance," Little Jake mumbled again, watching Wendell kick his cowpony into giving Freddie a hand.

Spinning Kasey around, he headed for a small stream. Kneeling beside the icy waters, he splashed water at his mouth and tongue, hoping to get rid of the fuzz. Gulping a mouthful of water, he swished it around and spat it out , hitting a frog on the head. "Bull's-eye! I'll bet that smart-aleck Freddie couldn't do that,"

Kasey was anxious to join her pals. She saw them disappearing over a rise and lunged forward as soon as Little Jake's foot hit the stirrup. This caused his other leg to skip along until he managed to bounce himself into the saddle.

He loosened the reins and Kasey went into an easy lope. Before they reached the herd, Little Jake brought Kasey up. He knew if he spooked the herd, he wouldn't be very popular with Rock Creek.

About half-way through the drive, Rock Creek directed the riders to make a large holding circle to give the mother cows and their calves time to find one another by scent - to 'mother-up'.

Rock Creek rode into the circle of milling bovines and quietly moved them around until they found each other. This helped to quieten the herd and they were soon moving uphill again.

Little Jake and his mom rode 'drag'*. This is where the less experienced help rode. It was very dusty at the back end and Little Jake sure didn't appreciate riding behind all those cow bums!

# ·⁺*Chapter 20·⁺*

The magic of the day was about to happen! They were nearing the old pine snag! Little Jake couldn't keep from grinning as he anticipated the big surprise in store for his mom and the buckaroos!

Moving at a snail's pace, Little Jake became more and more anxious. As he rode along, he'd been searching the aspen groves for a sign of Ki. Finally he spotted something darting between and under some deadfalls.

He stopped and stood up in his stirrups for a better look. "That's him! Thank goodness! Good old Ki!" He was so excited that he suddenly felt he had to pee, but he couldn't, not now! "Just what I needed!" he cringed, holding himself in.

The pressure under his belt subsided and he slumped back into his saddle. Ki was following the herd alright. A few of the cowdogs had spotted Ki and were tempted to give chase but they knew their masters wouldn't tolerate it. Being scolded by your master was the worst kind of humility a cowdog could ever suffer.

Little Jake was thankful for the well-trained cowdogs. By observing the cowdog's glances, he was able to keep track of Ki's whereabouts.

As the end of the herd passed the old pine snag, a 'herd quitter' and her calf veered off and ran down the hill. Little Jake knew that Ki was nearby.

This was the moment to put Ki into action!' He took a deep breath and whispered, "Ki, please don't let me down!" Fumbling for his dog whistle, he placed it between his lips and waited for the right moment.

His cheeks ballooned - the shriek of his whistle

pierced the air! Ki darted out of the aspens like 'greased lightning'! Surprised by the 'cowyote', the bewildered cow and calf spun around and doubled back to the herd in record time. Ki kept at their heels until they were past Little Jake. As quickly as he went to work for Little Jake, he disappeared!

Like it had been choreographed, the buckaroos, riding near the back of the herd, pulled up and skidded to a standstill! Their horses tensed. In unison, they stood up in their stirrups, stretching to see Ki dart back into the aspens. Their mouths wide open, they tried to figure out what had happened. They'd never seen a cow and calf return to the herd so quickly.

"What the heck happened!" hollered Wendell. Everywhere Little Jake looked, he saw astonishment and suspended animation.

The first to move was Rock Creek. He took off his hat and scratched his bald head. "Well, I'll be rode hard and put up wet!" he hollered. Spurring his cowpony out of its trance, he trotted over to where Little Jake and Kasey stood. They were watching Ki reappear on a hillside just above some aspens. He sat on his haunches as if he was awaiting Little Jake's next command.

"Why you sneaky rascal! You never told me you had a cowdog!"

"That's not a cowdog, Rock Creek! That's a 'cowyote' Little Jake said proudly.

"A Cowyote! Hmmm," Rock Creek thought for a moment and then said, Well, he's one hustlin' cowdog, if ever I've seen one! I'll be hog-tied!" he added, slapping his leg in delight.

"Little Jake! That was durned amazin'! I figgers, I jest figgered out why youse bin' actin' strange lately! I've gotta hand it to yuh, son! You shure pulled a dandy on us!" He took off his hat and once again scratched his bald head.

Little Jake's grin was so wide, it felt like his ears would touch. His special moment had arrived and had gone just as he'd planned! He had proven he could train his own cowdog! "Yee...! Haw! I'm a bonafide bucka-roo........!" he yelled, tossing his Stetson into the air.

It was Mom who rode up next. She had a proud look on her face. "Why Jake, you smarty pants, you even man-aged to keep your secret from me. Now I know why you were always in such a hurry to barrel out of the cook-house! I really am overwhelmed! How I wish your Grandpa was here to see this!"

Sidling up to Little Jake, she leaned out of her saddle, tousled his hair and gave him a big hug. Little Jake glowed with all the attention he was getting.

Everyone had fallen back into position to keep the herd moving. Little Jake could still see the buckaroos shaking their heads in disbelief. They kept twisting around in their saddles to take another look at the young 'marvel' in their midst.

"I sure pulled a good 'un on you guys, eh?" he rejoiced.

Throughout the rest of the turnout, Little Jake whis-tled commands to Ki to bring back 'herd quitters' a num-ber of times. Ki didn't let him down once! He was even faster and more proficient than most of the cowdogs. The buckaroos held their cowdogs back, just so they could watch Little Jake and Ki work. They kept shaking their heads in disbelief!

"Hey, Little Jake, he's a natural! Still cain't figger how you managed to train thet wild critter!" shouted Rock Creek, over the bawling herd. "Shure, be somethin' if'n yuh hauled him to a Stock Dog Competition. He'd be the champ fer shure!"

For a moment Little Jake imagined Ki taking the trophy and money at a Competition." The prize money could buy me that silverbelly and those hightop boots," he dreamed.

He reminded himself that Ki was a wild creature. "Could you imagine all the commotion he'd cause around all those other cowdogs," he thought. The setting of a competition was out of Ki's natural environment. It would never work. "And I'm sure I'd never be able to haul him around in a pickup! That's for shure!"

"Hey, Rock Creek! Guess what? One-Eye was Ki's first teacher."

"You must be kiddin'! You mean that old rascal had a coyote for a pal? This story jest gits more'n'more amazin'. Now that one I've gotta think on. This is sure beginnin' to sound like a tall tale to me."

"Honest, Rock Creek!" exclaimed Little Jake.

"Well, I always knew that One-Eye was special. Shure wish your Grandpa was here to see all o' this."

Ki's consistent performance throughout the 'Turnout', elated Little Jake. Even Kasey seemed to sense his pride and carried herself with showhorse elegance. She pranced up the trail like she had King Arthur on her back.

When they reached the high country pastures, the crew made a circle with their horses to get the calves to 'mother-up'. They would be left there until late fall to fill up on lush grass and grow fat.

It was dark by the time everyone returned to the Home Ranch. The main topic of conversation, all the way home, had been Little Jake and his amazing 'cowyote'.

Once back at the ranch house, Michelle had a quick

shower and disappeared into the ranch office, returning with a large envelope.

"Son, here's something special your Grandpa wanted you to have. It's something he arranged for in his will." Little Jake held his breath. He reached out, puzzling over what might be inside.

"What is it, Mom?" he asked, fumbling with the envelope. He ripped the envelope open and whooped,"It's a cheque, Mom! It's, it's a cheque!"

"Son, as we were riding home, Rock Creek and I decided you now have many of the qualities of a 'top-hand'! You've learned a lot in the last while... and then you amazed us with your 'cowyote'! What can I say," she said, giving her son a quick squeeze.

"I decided this would be a good time to let you have the envelope. I'm sure Grandpa would have agreed. He'd be right proud, Son!"

"Gee, thanks, Mom! And you too, Rock Creek!"

"Don't thank me, Son. Thank your Grandpa. And you did earn it. I'll look forward to you joinin' the crew more often now. Of course that's after your lessons and chores are done," he teased.

"Slitherin' snakes, Mom. There's enough here to get all that fine buckaroo gear I've always wanted! Can I spend it right away?"

"I've got the money put away in the Ranch account in Merritt, Jake. Grandpa made out a cheque to make sure you knew where the money came from," she winked.

Little Jake put the cheque to his chest, looked upward and said, "Thanks, Gramps! I sure do miss you!"

"Well, I guess we'd better head over to Andy's Saddle Shop tomorrow and do some shopping," added Michelle. Little Jake couldn't speak, all he managed to do was shake his head up and down. 🐑

# ^{{}^{\star}\!{}^{\star}}Chapter 21^{\star\,\star}

The sun was blazing into his bedroom when he awoke the next morning. Flipping over, trying to escape the glare, he spotted the cheque on his bedside table. "Holy cow! It wasn't a dream!" he cried.

Scampering over to his mom's bedroom, he crashed onto her bed and just about bounced her out. Still dazed she managed to grab a bedpost just in time to keep from falling out.

"Sheesh! Hold onto your halter, Jake! It's much too early to be up," she grumbled, clearing her throat and pulling her comforter over her head. "All my bones and my bum are still sore from yesterday's 'Turnout'. I'm sure Andy's won't be open 'til nine-thirty."

"But, Mom!" pleaded Little Jake, "it's already eight-thirty!"

"Oh, migosh! Pass me my watch. Eight-thirty, already! Okay, okay. Scoot! I'll get myself ready as fast as I can. We'll head over to the Quilchena Hotel for breakfast. Sharon's probably finished with breakfast and cleaned up already. How's that sound?" she asked.

That's great, Mom," said Little Jake, darting back to his bedroom.

Grandpa's pal, 'Stove-up Pete' and some of his other cronies were having breakfast at the Hotel, too. Little Jake was bursting to tell everyone about his 'cowyote'.

"I guess it would be too much like bragging," Little Jake decided. "Oh, well. I'm sure Rock Creek and the rest of the crew will 'let the pony out of the stall', soon enough."

\clubsuit91

They reached Andy's Saddle Shop just as Andy was stepping out of his pickup.

"Howdy", greeted Andy. "What are you two doin' in town so early? My, young fellah, do you ever look excited! I'm hoping and I'm a- guessin' you won the lottery. Right? Come on in. If'n you're that lucky, I'll do all I kin to help you spend it right here."

"You're right on the money, Andy! However this lottery was made possible by Little Jake's Grandpa," explained Michelle.

"I've come to get that silverbelly Stetson, Andy!" added Little Jake, full of anticipation.

"A buyin' buckaroo, first thing in the morning, really makes my day," returned Andy, as he fumbled and dropped his keys onto the porch, frustrating Little Jake's desire to get into the shop.

The door finally open, Andy slammed everything he was carrying onto a chair beside the door. He switched on the lights and reached for the silverbelly Stetson. Blowing the dust off its crown, he handed it to Little Jake.

Little Jake flung his old beat-up hat onto a nearby bench and eased the new hat onto his head, flashing his fingers across the brim, settling it on his head just right. He walked over to a mirror and admired his new lid.

It wasn't long before Little Jake was all decked out in a band collar shirt, new Levis', a notch-lapelled vest and to finish things off, Michelle knotted a bright red wild rag around his neck.

"Slow down, Mom!" he exclaimed. "I'm getting a sweat on just from pullin' on all these new duds. This is hard work," he joked, enjoying his shopping spree.

"Okay, time to take five!" suggested Andy. Your Mom and I will have a coffee. That'll give you a chance to stomp that outfit into place. And how about a hot chocolate for you, buckaroo?"

While they enjoyed their drinks, Michelle told Andy all about Little Jake's 'cowyote'. Andy just sat there with his mouth wide-open, letting his coffee get cold.

"Why, you're as slick as a greased piglet at a Fall Fair!" he grinned. "That is totally amazing! That one is goin' to take awhile to set up camp under my Stetson."

Still shaking his head in disbelief, Andy reached up on the boot rack and pulled down the pair of hightops that Little Jake had admired for so long. "I'll bet your feet have finally growed into them, Son. Even your cowpony will be proud to have you on board with these on," kidded Andy.

"Is there enough money to pay for them, too?" Little Jake asked his mom.

"You bet! "You know how much your Grandpa loved his high tops. He'd have wanted you to have the grandest pair around!"

As Little Jake stood up to wiggle his toes into his new hightops, he heard a jingle. Mom stretched out her hand and revealed a pair of shiny silver spurs.

"Too bad your dad isn't here to see your face, Son! I talked to him on the phone last night and told him about the trick you pulled on us. He laughed and laughed and then he said, "It sure sounds like he's earned his spurs, Michelle!" He wanted you to have these to show you how proud he is of your accomplishment.

Little Jake ran his finger across the engraved silver. "Did Bob from the Pooley Ranch make these? I know buckaroos that would trade their cowpony for these." He looked up to see his mom smiling. The sparkle in his eyes outshone his silver spurs!

As Mom and Little Jake were leaving, Andy handed him a horsehair hatband and matching stampede string.

"This is for that new silverbelly of yourn', Son! Wear it in good health. That's my gift to you for showing up those smart-alec buckaroos at the Double C. I'd have given away my best saddle to have seen the look on their ugly faces when that coyote turned back those bovines! Ho! Ho!" Andy chuckled, replaying the scene in his mind. "What a sight that musta bin'!"

Little Jake turned to give Andy a hug but he caught himself and instead stretched out his hand for a hand-shake. After all that was 'the buckaroo way'.

Leaving Andy waving off the porch of his Saddle Shop, they went downtown. While Mom stood in a line-up at the bank, Little Jake couldn't resist getting out of the pickup and showing off his new duds to anyone that happened by. He leaned casually against the pickup, pretending he wasn't paying any attention to all the admiring glances.

He overheard a couple of lady tourists say, "He's awfully young but he sure looks like a real cowboy to me. He must be from one of those big ranches in the Valley." That compliment made him stretch up like a giraffe - the buttons on his new shirt looked like they were about to pop.

Four hours later they were trailing a dust cloud into the Home Ranch. Even before Mom came to a stop, Little Jake bailed out and swaggered over to the the cookhouse, eager to show off his new outfit.

The buckaroos had just washed up and were strolling in for a late lunch.

"Hey, who's that dude a prancin' up the boardwalk?" teased Rock Creek.

"Yeh, looks like he's been shoppin' at The Bargain Barn," added Freddie.

"Nope, I'll bet he picked that outfit up at the Sally

Ann," interjected Pegasus.

Little Jake was crestfallen! Noticing that he was upset by all the teasing, Rock Creek walked over and put his hand on Little Jake's shoulder. "We're only teasin', Son! Jest betwixt you an' me we'd all give up our best cowponies to have yore outfit. And I mean that!"

Forty Mile sidled up on the other side and immediately tried to talk Little Jake out of his fancy spurs. Little Jake was feeling a lot better now.

"I'll give you my favourite headstall for those! You'd be gettin' the best part o' the deal! What say, buckaroo?"

"You throw in your best cowpony, Forty, and I'll think on it," Little Jake joshed back.

"Boy, you're shure one hard-nosed horse trader," returned Forty. Little Jake felt like a celebrity, now that everyone was hovering around and admiring instead of teasing. Although he knew he still had a lot to learn about being a buckaroo, he felt that he was finally being accepted by the crew.

It was about two weeks later, that he finished his research project on the burrowing owls. He rushed it over to show his mom. Just as he grabbed for the screen door, Rock Creek pulled it open, making him fall and drop his project on the floor.

Helping him pick it up, Rock Creek apologized and said, "Hey, pardner, haul yourself over to the horsebarn soon's yur finished here. I've got somethin' I wanna show yuh."

Little Jake was puzzled for a moment, but then said, "Okey dokey. I"ll be right over after Mom looks at my project."

"That's okay, Son. You go ahead. I'm kinda busy right now. I'll look at it first thing tomorrow morning," she assured.

Little Jake was even more confused now. He was also becoming suspicious because his mom had told him that she wanted to read the report as soon as it was finished.

"What's going on?" he wondered. "I hope this isn't one of Rock Creek's practical jokes."

As he left the office, he glanced over his shoulder and saw his mom coming too. Some of the buckaroos were also tagging along. Even Sharon, the cook, joined the parade.

"Boy! This must be something important! It's lucky that Mom's coming along. That way they won't try any 'funny stuff'," he reassured himself.

Just as he stepped through the barn door, Rock Creek disappeared into the tackroom and returned with something hidden behind his back.

"Turn around and close those peepers of yourn!" Rock Creek ordered. "Michelle, wrap this wild rag around his head, so's he cain't see, will ya?"

Little Jake began to fidget and worry. "Is this some kind of initiation to become part of the crew?" No one said a thing! It was dead quiet making him feel extremely uneasy.

Then he smelled new leather. He felt a belt being buckled around his waist and more buckling around his upper legs. That immediately gave away the surprise.

"Jeepers, a new pair of chinks!" hollered Little Jake jerking the wild rag off his face.

"Let the young colt loose," declared Rock Creek, giving a final yank on a leg strap. With the wild rag pulled down to his chin, Little Jake's eyes riveted on the fanciest pair of chinks he'd ever seen.

"Nothing but the best, for the ranch boss's son," Rock Creek winked at Michelle.

At a loss for words, Little Jake rushed to hug Rock

Creek but once again stopped short and put out his hand. He gave the firmest handshake he could muster. He pumped Rock Creek's hand so hard that he pretended to wince.

"Shure glad you like them, young fella! You'll put them to good use once I get you out on the range."

Two of the buckaroos hoisted Little Jake onto their shoulders and paraded him around the alley of the horse barn. He whooped and yahooed taking off his new Stetson and waving it around. Everyone in the barn clapped, whistled and cheered! Even the horses, in their stalls, added to the commotion by stomping around.

# ·*·*Chapter 22·*·*

All the excitement plumb wore Little Jake out. When he hit the bunk that evening, he slept like a hibernating bear. Next morning, he awoke with a long yawn and looked at the clock. He was shocked to find he had slept in.

Swinging his legs over the edge of his bunk, he shook his tousled head and blinked trying to get the sleep out of his eyes. He smelled new leather.

Looking down, he realized he'd worn his new chinks to bed! "Yeowzers! They even look good over my p.j.'s," he giggled.

He admired the silver conchos* and dragged the long fringes through his fingers. Putting his nose against the new leather, he sucked in the smell. "They smell good enough to eat," he giggled again. "Which reminds me, I guess I'd better get over to the cookhouse or I'll miss my breakfast."

Dressed in all his new finery, Little Jake swaggered over to the cookhouse. "I wonder what Ki will think of my new duds. Maybe he won't recognize me and make strange. Oh well, I'm sure he'll know who I am once he hears my voice," he concluded.

The cook house was empty. He remembered that it was Sharon's day off. All that sat on the carousel* were cereal boxes and condiments, like jams, honey, and so on. He filled his bowl with corn flakes and went to the fridge for milk. While there he searched for some 'cowyote' scraps. "Aha! Left-over breakfast bacon - right on!"

Wolfing down his cereal in record time, he skipped along toward the horse barn. Little Jake was feeling silly and decided to play a joke on Kasey. He pulled his wild rag over his nose as he came around the corner of the barn. Just as he'd hoped, Kasey was boogered.

"Ha! Ha! Fooled you. You sure are a scaredy-cat, Kase!" he chuckled, pulling the wild rag off his face. She snorted and side-stepped before she was convinced it really was Little Jake.

Soon they were loping across the meadows with Little Jake's red wild rag, blowing in the breeze. His new Stetson was tightly cinched on his head by a rawhide button on his new stampede string.

Just before they reached the old pine snag, Little Jake whistled to see if Ki was nearby. The unexpected shriek, made Kasey come to a sudden stop, causing Little Jake to lose his balance. He was catapulted onto Kasey's neck once again. Unable to hang on, he tumbled into the bunchgrass, crushing his brand new Stetson!

"Horse-feathers anyway, Kasey" he grumbled. He got up on one knee and tried to punch out the dented crown. "Whatcha do that for, you dumb horse?"

Reacting to Little Jake's angry tone, she side-stepped, nearly tromping on his foot. Little Jake rolled away just 'in the nick of time'. He jerked on the lead and muttered at her.

Picking up his new Stetson, he brushed gently at the crown, tears welling up in his eyes. "You know, Kasey. It's times like this that I'd like to ship you off to a glue factory." She responded by snorting and spraying Little Jake's Stetson with snot.

Ki had been perched on his mound watching intently and enjoying the 'cowboy comedy'.

Flicking the last few stems of grass from his hat, Little Jake lifted his head and saw Ki. He was awestruck!

Gamboling around Ki's legs were four cute, fuzzy

coyote pups! They were yelping, shoving, and tripping over each other.

"Holy Moley! Holy Mol—ey!" stammered Little Jake slumping onto the ground. "Migosh, Ki! You're not a boy - you're a-a-a-a girl ...a-a-a-a mom!"

Little Jake just sat there– his mouth wide open! All this time and he hadn't known that Ki was a girl! He was flabbergasted with Ki's litter of pups. He had been so busy with his 'cowyote' mission", he'd never once clued in.

"Ki, I"ve gotta tell you - you sure pulled a 'goodie' on me! How did you manage to keep those pups hidden for so long? You wily rascal, you!"

Little Jake quickly realized that Ki's natural instinct would have been to protect her newborn pups and therefore keep them sheltered and hidden until it was safe to reveal them.

"You know what, Ki? I came over today to show off my new buckaroo duds and instead you ended up 'stealing the show' by showing off your new family!"

Ki answered with a gentle howl and a pleased look across her snout. She sat patiently, but very alert, swishing her tail back and forth as the pups butted, scrambled and jockeyed for a gulp of milk.

"I sure can tell that you're one proud momma!" praised Little Jake.

# ·*Chapter 23·*·

As amazing as Ki's secret was, Little Jake was even more amazed when he realized that some of the pups had black and white colour tones. Those unnatural colours were mixed in with the natural coyote silver-greys! "That's very unusual!" he thought.

His eyes were drawn to one pup in particular! The one with milk covering his snout. Its belly obviously full, it became curious with Little Jake.

It walked to the front of the mound and sat on its haunches, closely observing his every move. He could tell it was a boy coyote. Trying to act ferocious, he let out a high-pitched yip. His face markings, although much lighter, were identical to One-Eye's. The shading around the eyes was definitely One-Eye!

Even Kasey became curious, stepping over, to gaze over Little Jake's shoulder at the writhing mass of fur. "Can you believe this, Kase? One-Eye and Ki were more than pals," he explained, turning to look up at her. "They were boy friend and girl friend, too! They were husband and wife! They were mom and dad!" Little Jake was so fascinated, he clamped his arms around his chest and didn't dare leave his vantage point.

"Holy rattlesnakes! This is incredible! Amazing! Wait 'til I tell, Mom!" he blurted, scaring the pups back into their den. They looked so comical, tumbling over each other, trying to be the first down the hole.

Within moments, tiny heads reappeared. The first pup out was the one resembling One-Eye. Right then and there, he decided he should be called One-Eye Junior.

Ki turned and began to lick the pup's head as if she was 'sprucing him up' for Little Jake. He ached to reach out and pet One-Eye Junior's soft fuzzy coat.

"What a legacy you've left, One-Eye! "Whatta good dog!" he whispered, so as not to scare away the pups.

"That patch of white around one eye and the patch of black framing the other, sure makes One-Eye your pa, alright!"

A loud yip from Ki made all of the pups disappear down into the hole again. "It must be 'nappy time', Kase," figured Little Jake, stepping up onto his cowpony. "It might be best to leave now. We'll be back tomorrow."

So delighted was Little Jake with his discovery, he raced and whooped all the way home! He couldn't wait to tell his mom and the buckaroos, especially Rock Creek. Little Jake knew the news would boggle his mind.

That night a full moon slipped up to sit on the edge of the horizon just as Little Jake crawled under Old Smelly. It was exceptionally bright outside.

"What a miracle!" he thought as he closed his eyes.

A coyote howled, popping Little Jake's eyes wide open. "I'll bet that was Ki!" Lying very still, he heard a chorus of high pitched yips.

"Boy, that sounds pretty close! I bet Ki's brought the pups down to show them where their pa used to live!"

One coyote pup's yip stood out. It was louder and longer than the rest. A big smile stretched across Little Jake's face. "I'll bet that's One-Eye Junior!

"Hey, boy! With the speed of your mom and the smarts of your pa, I'm gonna train you to be the best cow-dog in the whole Nicola Valley! And Gramps - that's a promise!"

# ·⁺*Epilogue·⁺*

..............In the days after this story, a special poem was made up around the campfire to celebrate Little Jake's amazing accomplishment!

Cowboy campfires are a lot of fun and Little Jake loved it when his mom let him join the buckaroos. They did rope tricks, sang and yodelled cowboy songs. They also told tall tales and recited cowboy poetry.

Each buckaroo and even Little Jake's Mom created a line for the poem. Here's the poem!

## LITTLE JAKE'S COWDOG

Little Jake wanted his very own cowdog - real bad
He wanted to be a buckaroo - just like his Grandad

But, Little Jake, you're too little to train one
And I'm too busy - I've got the Double C to run

In a few years - down the trail, maybe
Play with One-Eye for now - then we'll see

Now Little Jake - he didn't let on
But he had a secret a' brewin' and was havin' fun

He'd found a coyote up in the Upper Meadow hills
Spent hours ridin' out there - tryin' his cowdog trainin' skills

Now that coyote became his 'cowyote' - you see
He was the smartest and fastest on the Double C

It was 'spring turnout' - when he let him loose
The surprised cowboy crew - almost swallowed their snoose

But then Little Jake got a surprise - all his own
The 'cowyote' was a momma - One-Eye's fame had grown

A herd of frisky pups- seemed to appear out of nowhere
One was the spittin' image of One-Eye
Yup, he was definitely, his heir!

# JAKE'S SADDLEBAG OF BUCKAROO WORDS:

1. boogered - frightened / spooked
2. buckaroo - (from Spanish vaquero) cowboy
3. buckarette - cowgirl
4. carousel - round wheel on dining table top which is turned to reach such things as salt, jams, ketchup, etc.
5. cantle - the raised rear part of the saddle seat
6. concho - knobs of silver used to decorate buckaroo gear and tack
7. deadfall - a tree knocked down by high winds
8. drag - rear part of cattle drive; watched by junior cowhands
9. drive - cattle gathered into a herd for moving to another location.
10. duds - clothes a buckaroo, cowboy / cowgirl wears.
11. fender - part of saddle / leather shields hanging between rider's legs and horse
12. galoot - a hombre (bad, tough character)
13. ground-tied - a horse trained to stand still when the reins are dropped to the ground
14. gumbo - muddy clay / very sticky and

slippery
15. hoolihan - a quiet rope throw to catch a horse
16. keester - a person's bum
17. mecate - horse hair braided to make a lead rope and reins
18. mother-up - a calf and mother cow finding each other by scent
19. overgrazing - cows eating down a pasture so grass doesn't regrow
20. out of the red - a ranch that still makes money
21. popper - leather piece on the end of mecate lead used to hit horse on the rump to make it go faster
22. rollers - snorting sound made by spooked horse
23. snoose - chewing tobacco
24. snubbing post - a post in the middle of a corral to tie a horse to
25. spring turnout - a time cows and calves are driven to the high country for summer pasturing
26. stove-up - old cowboys limping from injuries they got being cowboys
27. toolies - brushy/treed country
28. turnback - a calf/cow wanting to go back home while on a drive
29. undershot - a tall cowboy boot heel slanted under to keep foot from sliding through stirrup
30. wallow - a hole dug by bulls so that they can kick up dust to get rid of flies
31. wild rag - bandana/scarf
32. windy - a tall tale
33. wreck - an accident on horseback
34. yodel - a special singing sound in cowboy songs

# Yeppasiree! I'm a buckaroo!